Riley

by Michelle Woody

iUniverse, Inc.
New York   Bloomington

Riley
Copyright © 2010 by Michelle Woody

All rights reserved. No part of this book may be used or reproduced by any means, graphic, electronic, or mechanical, including photocopying, recording, taping or by any information storage retrieval system without the written permission of the publisher except in the case of brief quotations embodied in critical articles and reviews.

iUniverse books may be ordered through booksellers or by contacting:

iUniverse
1663 Liberty Drive
Bloomington, IN 47403
www.iuniverse.com
1-800-Authors (1-800-288-4677)

Because of the dynamic nature of the Internet, any Web addresses or links contained in this book may have changed since publication and may no longer be valid. This is a work of fiction. All of the characters, names, incidents, organizations, and dialogue in this novel are either the products of the author's imagination or are used fictitiously.

ISBN: 978-1-4502-1933-4 (pbk)
ISBN: 978-1-4502-1934-1 (ebk)
ISBN: 978-1-4502-1932-7 (hbk)

Printed in the United States of America
iUniverse rev. date: 3/15/10

Chapters

1. Good Day / Good Night — 1
2. Charley Arrives — 7
3. Meeting Charley — 15
4. Tom — 28
5. Riley's Rough Week — 34
6. Greg's Surprise — 46
7. Weekend with Greg — 52
8. A Clown's Birthday Party — 64
9. Rennick's Irritation — 72
10. Meeting the Devil — 79
11. A Belief About Greg — 88
12. The Specialness of Tom — 90
13. A Healing Afternoon — 99
14. Annette's Advice — 110
15. Charley's Magic — 115
16. Much More — 120
17. The Last Time — 130
18. Leftovers From Charley — 135
19. Riley's Bad Night — 140
20. Charley's Magic for Riley — 147

21. Tuesday	164
22. The Hospital	171
23. Rennick's Confession	176
24. Dinner at Charley's	179
25. Tornado	183
26. Bachelor Auction	190
27. One Found, One Lost	195
28. The Funeral and the Lovers	201
29. Riley's Family	208
30. Greg's Goodbye	215
31. Making Hay	219
32. The Auction	224
33. Riley's Odd Little Town	229

Good Day / Good Night

Mayor Riley Halleran knew his day would be bad by the sight on the flagpole in the town square. A pair of camouflage pants hung on the pole instead of the flag.

"He strikes again," he sighed, shaking his head.

Tempted to turn around and go back home, Riley parked in his reserved spot by the City Hall. The building was more ornate than the others by it, but it was still a simple, two-story brick building that faced the south side of the square.

Riley grabbed his bag and left his truck. A strong wind blew through his short dark hair, making him regret wasting so much time on his appearance that morning. He could hear the ropes of the flagpole clanking as the wind tossed the pants around but he couldn't bring himself to look at the sight. His attention lay ahead of him at the police chief that was obviously waiting for him. Kevin Russell stepped outside, walking towards him.

Russell was taller and a few years older than Riley and possessed a complete look of intimidation. While Riley lacked the seriousness Kevin carried, the two were often mistaken for brothers. They had been friends even before he became Mayor.

Riley offered him a sympathetic smile.

"You seen him?" the chief asked, his voice deep and gruff with his authority.

"Not recently." He stood next to the chief as they looked back at the flagpole. "Wonder what he's upset about now?"

"We'll ask him when we find him. Also soaped the windows at the tractor supply store and the benches are missing in the park." Chief Russell's face then cracked with the smile Riley preferred to see.

Riley smiled too. "Well, I doubt the benches went far. Let me know when you find him; if I need to make bail."

"Will do," Kevin nodded and walked away.

There was an unexpected irritation in Riley then as he walked to his office. There was too much importance placed on that day and he didn't want to think of how many ways it could go horribly wrong. Pants on the flagpole was a good start.

Riley's office was on the second floor with a view of the beautiful town. His secretary Lana sat in the waiting area, handling guests and tasks for his office and the city manager in the office next to his.

She stood when he walked in. Lana Clease was a delicate young woman, deeply religious and the most open-minded person as well. That was probably why Riley liked her so much. She was a friend, kept his office running efficiently and could offer a prayer or a curse, depending on the situation. That morning, she waited with an anxious smile and a stack of messages.

"I see he's been busy," he said, stopping at her desk to skim the messages.

"I checked with the sheriff. They haven't gotten him yet but I guess he hit four flag poles."

"And soaped windows and took the park benches," he nodded. "I met the Chief downstairs." He started towards his office, almost afraid to enter the realm of it.

"I'll put them through if they call," Lana was saying as he stepped into the quiet office.

"Thanks." That problem would have to wait, though. Riley had bigger issues on hand than flags and park benches that day.

He'd orchestrated a tour of their empty factory in town for a big-money corporation in the nearby city. If the company took the deal it would offer the town some financial hope. If they didn't, the town would still be in financial despair with a bankrupt factory and Riley would be out all the hours and politicking it'd taken to simply arrange the tour.

He had two more hours to nervously prepare to woo the men coming and two more hours for the whole deal to fall through.

The sun was going down, giving Riley an awesome view of the sky on fire from his front porch. He'd been home less than an hour. He'd fed all the animals and grabbed a snack for himself, his stomach still not ready for food. He knew the town was celebrating, perhaps individually in the home of every person who had found a job that day. The bankers were running the numbers of the deal and congratulating themselves. The deal would be hitting the local news of a small town revived. And the creator of the whole spectacular deal sat on the front deck of his home, stressing over the lunch tab.

He barely paid attention to the sounds of the woods before him or his farm around him. He didn't feel the joy he'd expected. His mind was tied up with so many thoughts ranging from good to bad that not much touched him that warm evening.

It was the sound of a car approaching that broke him from his prison of thoughts. From where he sat on the porch he couldn't see his driveway but he knew the sound of the expensive sedan being cautiously driven down the gravel drive. He hadn't expected Greg to visit that night but the surprise visit of his lover met with the same distance as everything else had that day.

He heard the door shut and then Greg Robins soon came into view. He was dressed in jeans and a nice sweater. Greg was a news anchor for a station in the city. He'd been voted the city's favorite for two years in a row. He was sexy with an athletic build. He was aging into a distinguished man, his sandy blond hair still full but Riley could see gray in there occasionally.

Riley looked at him, offering a smile, a hello, but didn't leave his place.

Greg sat on the steps beside him. "What are you doin' here? Should be celebrating, not moping." Greg's voice was deep, his words crisp with years of training for public speaking.

Riley nodded, aware that if Greg knew he should be celebrating then it had made the news. "I should be but I paid for lunch. $75.00 and not sure where gonna get it."

"Bill the town," Greg casually offered.

"We don't have it either." Riley took a bite of his carrot and then threw the rest of it into the woods. His Siamese cat Savannah took off chasing it.

"You look tired," Greg said gently.

It made Riley smile but he offered no other response.

Greg moved to sit behind him, putting Riley between his legs. His strong hands went to Riley's shoulders and began massaging them, forcing the muscles there to relax whether they wanted to or not. "You're so tense."

"It was a tense day," he said, wincing through Greg's attack on his back.

"You realize you just employed 90% of your town today."

"86.3, actually," Riley reported.

"Ask for a raise."

"Right. $1.00 an hour?"

"You offered part of your salary to help the town out. Ask for some help back. Nothing wrong with that. You just made the town a fortune. Let the town share."

"Too much hassle." Riley had to admit the massage was helping him let go of his worry.

They sat there for a few minutes more, Greg massaging his back but not so forcibly. He was beginning to let the massage totally take away his thoughts when Greg leaned up and kissed his neck, gently biting him, a clear telling of what he was thinking.

"I'm not in the mood," he sighed, still burdened by what check was going to bounce first.

"I can give you the seventy-five," Greg said, stopping his actions and leaning close to him to show he was serious. He slid his hands around Riley's body, holding him. "Hell, I'll give you seventy-six," he said, his fingers going to the buttons on Riley's shirt. "There, you got a raise."

"Greg," Riley sighed but not really fighting the unbuttoning of his shirt.

"I'll give you eighty if you take the shirt off." Greg moved to sit more at Riley's side, focused on unbuttoning the shirt. "Eighty-one to bite that gorgeous chest." Greg's eyes were alight with his new game.

Riley had to admit it was making him forget about his troubles, although they were trying to remain his focus.

"This negotiating is hot," Greg said, kissing his neck and moving to his lips. "We'll have to do this again," he said, making contact on Riley's mouth.

Greg ran his tongue over Riley's lips. He moved to sit over Riley, gently laying him back to the deck. Their kiss continued hungrily until Riley broke away.

"Okay," he said, "inside. I don't want to be on the front page making out."

"Alright," Greg said. He stood up, the bulge in his jeans obvious. He offered Riley his hand and helped him up. "Eighty-six for sex on the sofa," Greg continued with a sly smile. "Ninety-five if you do me. One hundred if I do you."

"Please," Riley smiled, embarrassed but secretly loving it.

Inside the door, they were back to kissing. Greg quickly removed Riley's open shirt then began unzipping his pants while Riley undid Greg's. Quickly the clothes were left in piles on the living room floor as they moved to the sofa.

Charley Arrives

Riley rolled over in his sleep, sliding his hand over the side of the bed, expecting to reach out and touch Greg's warm body. He found only the chill of an empty side. He opened his eyes, finding Greg up and dressing. "You're leaving?"

"Got a long drive and still have to get ready for work."

"Could stay," Riley said, smiling dreamily at the man he loved.

"I've got to work."

"Move-in stay."

Greg continued dressing, not giving Riley a response.

"Had you up to one-fifty last night. Not worth staying?"

"Sorry," Greg sat on the bed beside him, kissing him. "I've got to go."

Riley watched him leave, feeling lonely and that perhaps the talk they kept avoiding was being avoided because Riley knew he'd lose Greg when he pressed him. "Love you, too," he said after the door shut. "Damn."

With a call to the bank that morning, Riley hoped that he could get his checks covered long enough to not be impeached.

What he found out only troubled him, finding his account had over a thousand dollars in it.

He dealt with his morning stuff quickly then he made a call to Greg.

"Greg Robins."

"It's me. I just found out my bank balance is off. An employee there recognized the culprit though. Said he was on the news."

"Really? Did we do a story on him?" Greg asked with such seriousness that Riley wasn't sure he knew what he meant.

"Why did you do that?"

"Why not?" Greg's tone changed from the professional Greg to the sweet man Riley loved.

"It's too much."

"No. Keep it. It's nothing. Come on, you need it. I know it. Let me help you. It's a gift for negotiating a million dollar deal for your town."

Riley couldn't deny he needed the money but he hated taking it too. Part of him wondered if it wasn't just hush money. Paranoid thoughts, sure, but they were there. "I'll pay you back."

"Nonsense. Consider it me helping out around there, just as if I was cleaning stables or cuttin' hay, things I can't do. I can do this."

Riley sighed. Perhaps he was resisting it because he wanted to hear the right words, the I'm-helping-because-I-love-you words.

The town of Sleeper wasn't really the average, quiet small town. It had its share of trouble, keeping the police chief and his crew busy. There were the oddballs that kept the norm just a step off and there were the regular folk just trying to raise families and do an honest day's work. Most of the time, Riley felt like the babysitter, having learned quickly that the title of Mayor meant having to settle some disputes, listen to the troubles and to keep some of the insanity from ever crossing the police chief's desk. He'd been the youngest mayor elected there and in his years, he'd been involved in his fair share of town's issues.

But Riley called the town home, oddballs and all. He felt comfortable there and generally the town meetings were never places for heated battles or troubles. The town ran fairly quietly. While Riley fussed every time something irritating happened (like the school band marching repeatedly around the town square to protest the yearbook's delay) he knew he'd miss the uniqueness there if it ever left. He lived in the Twilight Zone town where the normal and different met and melded - peacefully.

Yet while the town was accepting and knew its reputation of being so, there was still a shockwave ripple through town the day *he* arrived.

After his stressful morning of worrying about money and then looking foolish at the bank for not knowing he *had* money, Riley decided to treat himself to lunch at the café, where he was part of the regular group. Usually he just got a salad and soda but that day was broccoli - cheese casserole made by the owner's wife Linda and it wasn't something Riley thought he could pass up.

While the lunch time was usually busy there, that day it was alive. The group at the bar was hanging on Linda's every word.

Again Riley felt foolish. "What's going on?" he asked, amazed at the group's interest. Something had them afire.

"You haven't heard?" Bill Gasten asked. Bill and Riley had gone to school together and hadn't ever really been friends until about five years after school and Bill let go of his macho football ego and realized that Riley wasn't after him. They were social friends only because they had never moved to really being buddies. Riley had no interest in hunting and Bill had no interest in horses.

"A celebrity bought Ellen's ranch," Linda said, smiling big as the spotlight was on her once again.

"Really? Who?" he asked, not aware that the next sentence would have been words never spoken in that town.

"A dragon," she said with emphasis on the word like it meant something.

It only made Riley unsure he'd heard her right. "A dragon?" He looked at the small collection of audience around him and saw the same amazement on their faces as Linda's. Quickly running through his limited knowledge of slang and words that Linda wouldn't have known, he came up with nothing more than a mythical beast. "Dragon?"

"She's really a man," Earl Blake explained.

"Oh! Drag queen," Riley said.

"Well, whatever the word is," Linda said, trying to hide her embarrassment. "She bought the place and moved in last night."

"Who is it?" Riley asked, trying to run through celebrity drag queens that Linda might have heard of and that the town would be interested in.

"Charley Claremont," Linda said, her smile then from her joy that Charley was actually there.

Charley Claremont as his feminine persona Miss Charley had a cooking / talk show that had attracted celebrities and the attention of the general public. Perhaps some didn't really know that he was a man dressed like a woman or some just believed it was all a character he'd made to spoof the regular talk shows but Charley had become a sensation. He was on all the covers, had cook books out, had a stand-up comedy routine that toured the world and moved among the celebrity circle of paparazzi and gossip. Funny as hell and an even better cook.

Riley had been a fan of Charley's since his early beginnings, before the cooking shows. He had several concert DVDs and had watched Charley's shows every week when he could afford to have satellite. Charley was handsome as a man and good-looking as a woman. He was popular for his intelligent humor and also his compassion. Riley had always thought of Charley as a Mom baking cookies with her family, her guests.

And Charley had found his way to Riley's small town. That fact made Riley curious. It didn't seem to trouble any of the others there. They were so excited to have such a celebrity in their midst. Riley loved his town, he really did, but the fact that a world-wide phenomenon star had settled in a town that probably wasn't on some maps seemed almost impossible.

Linda and the group continued the frenzied talk about Charley and what they'd heard or seen so far. Riley seemed to be the only one who thought this fact was weird.

Leaving the café, and walking back to work, Riley saw the celebrity for himself. Charley was leaving his Pacifica, headed down the sidewalk, perhaps to the café to cause a commotion that Riley would hear about for days. He wore a coat of bright orange and pink with fur cuffs and a large pink hat. A small purse swung from his arm. There was a distinct feminine walk to his hurried pace, despite the high heels. He didn't appear to see Riley.

It was only after Charley stepped into the café that Riley was aware he had stopped and watched the complete movement from car to café.

"Looks like a hippie pimp," Chief Russell's voice said from Riley's side, startling him.

"Quite something," Riley nodded, feeling as if he'd just witnessed a tornado move through the center of town. How one person could demand such attention was amazing. "Must be our celebrity."

Kevin smiled at him. "Just what our town needed, huh?" He shrugged and started walking on. "Oh," he said, turning to face Riley and walking backwards, "he's in there." Kevin nodded back towards the jail. "They caught him this morning."

Rennick Halleran had been an outspoken lawyer in his day. He'd been to every war protest and every environmental action he could attend. In his forty-some years as being the voice of law and reason, Rennick had served whatever good purpose, doing whatever he felt was needed.

That fire in him had continued even after his retirement, which to Riley's chagrin had given him more free time to act upon the wrongs. In Riley's oddball town, his own father was one of the shining stars.

Jail time didn't trouble Rennick. It was a reward to him almost, letting him know his actions had been noted. That day, he sat in the cell, joking with Gerald Tristan, the officer watching over the jail.

Stress had defined Rennick's aging body. Riley had his dark hair, strong build and ice-blue eyes but still possessed the youthfulness. Putting the two together, it was obvious they were father and son. Riley looked like his dad. He saw nothing in him that resembled his mother physically. He had only adopted her gentle nature and not his dad's activism. Perhaps that was what had separated Riley and his dad all those years. He had been a disappointment to his dad the way his dad had been a thorn in his side.

Gerald stood as Riley entered the jail. "Mayor Halleran," he said, his voice soft despite the huge muscle-mass of a man he was. Riley didn't know if the formal title came from respect or from Gerald's siding with Rennick. Who knew what horrible things his dad had said. "There's no bail amount this time," Gerald said. "You'll just have to sign for him. Any trouble, we come for you too."

He looked at his dad, knowing he'd have to sign that paper despite a huge fear that he'd be spending his first night in jail. His well-being wasn't going to be concern enough for his father to act right.

"How long's that contract binding?" Rennick asked, as Riley signed.

Gerald shrugged. "Whatever Chief wants, I suppose." He grabbed the key and moved to let Rennick out.

Riley watched with the familiarity of the whole scene with no idea how many times they'd done that.

Rennick shook Gerald's hand, then patted the officer on the arm. "I guess we'll both be seeing you tomorrow and we can finish this talk then."

"Alright, Ren."

Riley didn't say anything, hoping his dad was just trying to unnerve him. He remained quiet as they left the jail and went outside. He felt the need to escort his father to the free world and ensure that he didn't insult a judge before he left the courthouse just to get them arrested.

There was an anger growing inside him that he wanted to vent at his dad. It was his dignity and freedom on the line now as well. But he kept his irritation contained. "Try to not get into trouble for a while, okay? Not even the slightest little thing."

"I'll try," Rennick smiled, nodding, but he was shitting him. Riley knew it.

"Dad, I'm serious. This affects me, you know."

Rennick looked down then out at something moving in the town behind Riley. "I'd sure hate for the mayor to have to claim an outcast." He walked away from Riley, leaving the same frustration he always did.

Riley let him go, putting his hand at his temple to try to stop the throbbing that was beginning.

"Hey, Rile?" his dad called back.

He turned to look at his dad, expecting more words of defiance or irritation.

"Good job on ole Miller's factory. He'd be honored to know that place was alive again. That was his pride and joy. Good job."

Surprised by the praise, Riley was slow to respond. "Well, thanks."

Rennick nodded and turned and walked away.

Riley noticed then that Charley's Pacifica was driving by, the celebrity no doubt having been watching the sidewalk encounter between Riley and Rennick and he knew then what his dad had been watching behind him. He watched the car move on by and then decided he should have waved, as frustrated with the celebrity's watching as he was with the chaos that his father had created for him that day.

Meeting Charley

The fact that it was Saturday didn't ease Riley's troubles. Monday would be coming back around soon enough. And that was only if trouble didn't come to him before that - depending on which neighbor had a concern or what his father did.

It was his horse Scarecrow that he sought out that morning. No matter how much life troubled him, Riley could count on his horses to ease his troubles, but even that day, Scarecrow was giving him grief. The horse refused to stand still, nudging him and turning back to look at him as he threw the saddle over the horse's back.

But once they left the barn for the freedom of the open fields, horse and rider became one, enjoying the run and eventually the walk through the beautiful countryside.

Riley's relaxing ride came to an abrupt end as they rode up onto the road and one turn away sat a Pacifica at the side of the road.

The driver was unique to that town and that radiated from the man standing beside the vehicle, wearing black leather pants, a pink camo top and black high heel boots. His natural, short blond hair was neatly styled. He wore dark fingernail polish that

Riley could see from his distance and a scaled down version of the makeup. Except for the heels, Riley saw a strong, tall man.

Charley was clearly focused on trying to get a signal on his phone, seemingly unaware of Riley's approach. He put his hand on his hip, giving his phone attitude. "I should just throw you into the woods!" he said, his voice getting louder as he spoke. Only then did he turn and see Riley. His mood changed instantly, "Well, if it isn't my knight in shining armor," he smiled, the phone being slid into his pocket. "Minus the armor." Charley slid his yellow-lensed sunglasses down a bit as if taking a better look at Riley.

Riley stopped Scarecrow near the car, "What happened?"

"The tire just blew and I absolutely have no idea how to change one if I could and my phone has no signal at all."

"That's normal for phones out here. Have to be on top of the hill."

"Figures," Charley looked to the distant hill, biting his bottom lip then sighing like it was too great a distance to even consider walking.

"I can change it if you have a spare," Riley offered, feeling obligated to offer. He smiled at Charley's obvious frustration. "It'll get you to town at least but you'll have to get the other one fixed if you're going to be driving these roads all the time."

"You would be a life saver," he said, a tone to his words like he felt embarrassed at his situation.

Riley dismounted then led Scarecrow to the side of the road. He unhooked the reins then let him go. The horse went to graze as Riley walked back to Charley. "I'm Riley Halleran by the way," offering his hand more out of habit than formality.

"I know," Charley smiled, shaking Riley's hand with a soft touch. "I saw you in town yesterday. I'm Charley Claremont," he nodded, his expressive eyes gleaming.

"Yes. The whole town's talking about you being here."

"I bet they are. I do tend to make people talk. But I'd have it no other way," he said as if confessing a secret.

"I sorta gathered that," Riley smiled, taking in Charley's outfit. He went about getting the jack and tire out.

"I can't tell you how relieved I am to have some help. I was beginning to imagine all sorts of horrible happenings out here. Heels are a bitch to run in on gravel."

"I imagine. I don't think you'd have any trouble, at least I'd like to think so. Not until dark, anyway," he added, merely for the tease. "What brings you to Sleeper? Can't imagine we're a real hotspot for celebrities."

"That's one bonus," Charley nodded. "I had to get away from that world for a while. I needed some place to escape and I doubt I'd be found here." Charley moved with Riley as he moved to the flat tire. "I just searched for property for sale online. This place sounded perfect and I saw it and fell in love. And, I'd heard a lot about the town's gay mayor."

"Oh," Riley caught his breath, Charley's words filling him with all kinds of worries. How could it have been about him? There was also a flare up of being ambushed out there but he quashed that fear quickly. "I'm afraid to ask what you've heard." He concentrated on the lug nuts of the wheel, mentally praying that he could loosen them and not look weak.

Charley took off in what sounded like an introduction for his show, "The young mayor who commonly sports a few days growth of beard, listens to rock to classical, openly gay and been re-elected twice in the small town that's seen a 20% increase in revenue until the deal this week which sent that out of the water and a 5% increase in population. He also voted himself a 5% decrease in salary, turning the money over to town employees for their raises. He's worked on farm legislature and recently landed a big-time contract with a factory in town, which is all the town talks about right now, by the way."

"Wow," he smiled, uncomfortable, "I feel like I've been researched."

"I just thought you'd make a great guest on my show. A regular guy doing spectacular things for his town. Might influence some politicians in this country that seem to have forgotten what it's all about."

"I'm not out to change the world."

"You should be," Charley said with a serious tone. "You'd be able to do it. You're trustworthy. Cute. Young. Sensible. Know how to change a tire."

He smiled, keeping his focus on the task before him. He was aware how comfortable it felt to talk to the man he didn't know. He'd have to be careful what he let himself say. "Well, it was just me and my mom growing up. Someone had to handle to awful jobs."

"You have a farm near here, huh?"

"I do. I'm afraid to ask what you know about that," he looked up at Charley quickly then back to the tire.

Charley smiled. "What I don't know is if you're single."

"I'm with someone," he said, aware he'd spoken up quickly. Perhaps too quick.

"Someone in town?"

"No. He lives in the city." Instantly, Greg wasn't a subject he wanted to discuss with the celebrity at his side.

"Ooh, long distance relationship then. Interesting. I'd be interested to meet him."

Riley kept his eyes on the tire as he set it, aware there would be no way he'd ever get Greg to meet Charley. Greg was about secrets and Charley was about exposure.

Perhaps Charley understood that in his non-response.

Charley left Riley's view, going to the driver's side and opening the back door. Riley could hear him doing something that sounded like getting something from a cooler and then the door was shut. Charley returned to his side, drinking from a water bottle and another one in hand that was for Riley.

"I do want you to consider being on my show. It would be great publicity for your town. Might start a tourist flow and that's always good for the bottom dollar."

"Thanks, but I have issues with stage fright and that's just too terrifying to even consider."

"It's taped." Charley then squatted down so his face was at Riley's level. "We could shoot it at your house, even," he reported, his expression alive with his new idea. "Be just us and the crew. All we'll do is cook and talk like we are now. No tours of the house, I promise. You're my guest and I won't treat you wrong."

"I don't doubt that."

"Think about it. Don't worry. Just think about the good outcomes. I'll be here for a couple of months. Let me know before then."

"You're not going to take no for an answer, are you," he said, seeing the set-up. "I'll think about it."

"Thank you." Charley took a drink, like drinking to victory, and then asked, "Do you think I could get you and your man to come to dinner one night soon? I love to cook for people and I owe you big time for this."

"You don't owe me, really," he said, hoping to close the subject.

"Is that a no as well?"

Riley tried to think of a smooth answer to get out of that but he couldn't find the right way. "I doubt he'd go to dinner, honestly."

"Why? Because of me?"

"No. Because he doesn't want anyone to know he's with a man and, well, you'd be too much of a risk I'd say." He regretted saying that the moment the words formed but he couldn't take them back.

"He's hiding?" Charley about lost his balance as he reacted. "How old is he?"

"He's hiding, yes. He's married." Riley answered the questions with a bit of protective anger but the words were true.

Charley let out a whoop. "You are involved with a married man who is choosing this secret life over being with you?"

Riley didn't want to answer.

"Oh honey, I would never keep you a secret. I've got to meet him now."

He tried to get the lug nuts tightened faster, feeling an urgency to leave.

"Is he someone important? The mayor there?"

"No. Nothing like that. Look, I don't want to defend our lives to you. We have what we have."

"Are you happy with that?" Charley dared.

Riley looked at him and then away, deciding not to continue the talk. "You don't owe me for the tire, let's leave it at that."

"Avoidance. Not a good sign."

Riley sighed, trying to collect his thoughts. "Is this what you do to your guests? We're going to be arguing about my life?"

"No. I just ask questions. It's what I do. So that means you'll be on my show?"

"No, I'm not going to be on your show."

"Oh yeah. A mayor with secrets doesn't do talk shows."

"I don't have any secrets," Riley said, meeting Charley's eyes.

"That's right. Your man does. He's either not very happy or not very smart."

He paused, letting that thought settle before he spoke. "That may be," Riley confessed, looking back at the tire, knowing he felt Charley's statement was true. "But it's what I got."

Charley nodded, humming a bit. "So I'm right, you're not happy."

Riley looked away from him, almost dropping the tire iron in his embarrassment. "Let's just not talk about me anymore, okay? Tell me some celebrity story. I'm almost done here. You can go on to town and bother someone there."

"Oh, I plan to," his serious tone gone, his eyes wide with his joy. "I have a mission." Charley stood up, taking a drink of water.

"No you don't," Riley stood up. "Don't you do anything to hurt him."

Charley studied him. He had a small handkerchief that he dabbed his forehead with before he spoke. "I won't do anything. It's for my own knowledge. I have to know who this man is that you're in love with. And then I'm going to go to his house and face him and tell him he's a big fool for hurting you."

He was silenced by Charley's response. What he wouldn't have given to have Greg acknowledge their relationship and his love.

Charley handed over the bottle of water he'd been holding like a peace offering. "You need this. It's ice cold. I always have something cold to drink wherever I am. Usually champagne or such, but today it's water. Thank you for helping me and I won't go after him, but I'd like to and I think a bit of you would like me to. But that's okay. I give you my word I won't do anything. I'm just curious about my sexy mayor I've been wanting to meet for a long time. Curious about the man that owns you."

Riley looked away, unsure how he wanted to respond to Charley's words. "And you? Single or some out-there relationship that everyone knows about?"

"No. I'm single. Men find me intimidating."

"Humph." Riley moved to put the tire iron and jack back in their places. He sat his water down and then went to get the tire. He rolled it to the trunk and put it in. "You'll want to get that fixed soon. The spare won't last long out here."

"Thank you. Any place good in town?"

"The gas station by the bank at the four-way stop."

"Thank you."

"You're welcome. Thanks for the water."

Charley nodded. "Can I fix you dinner tonight?"

"Well, I have plans already. Sorry."

"With Mystery Man?"

Riley smiled, looking away from Charley.

Charley sighed. "Sorry if I said something wrong. I do that. I don't think about what I say. I won't do anything to hurt you. Really, I am sorry. Please think about being on my show. We won't discuss anything but politics, I swear."

"I doubt I could out-debate you on that subject either."

Charley cocked his head to the side, smiling, "Probably right," he smiled. "Riley Halleran, it has been a pleasure to meet you and I thank you forever for saving me today."

"You're welcome," Riley simply said. He looked towards Scarecrow and whistled softly. The horse shook his head then walked close enough for Riley to hook the reins. The horse moved his head down to Riley's shoulder, like he was giving a hug. Riley patted Scarecrow's nose, realizing he had one ally on his side. Scarecrow's love was unconditional. "I'll see you around," he said to Charley and moved to the horse's side while Charley stepped around the car to the driver's door. He climbed into the saddle as Charley started the car. He waited and watched as Charley drove away, a hand out the window to wave good-bye. He was left with a mixture of feelings about the encounter and not too many of them ones that he was comfortable with.

There was one person who knew Greg's secret. Well, to a degree. Greg's brother Matt was a doctor in the city and was hardly ever home. He let his baby brother use his home to meet his lover. Matt had no problem with Greg's affair but Matt didn't know it was a man Greg was meeting.

Greg never bothered to correct Matt's assumption.

It was Matt's house that Riley drove to that night. The lights were on in the house so he knew Greg was there. Greg's car would be in the garage. Riley sometimes parked in the garage as well to hide his entrance into the house but since it was dark already, he parked in the drive and went to the door, letting himself in.

There was a nice piano song playing through the living room. Candles were lit randomly throughout the living room and dining room. The table was set but Riley doubted they'd be eating. Greg wasn't known for his cooking and if they had anything, it would be a cake or pie he'd bought.

Greg joined Riley's side in the dining room, offering him a glass of wine and a light kiss. He wore jeans and a button-down shirt that was buttoned only so far up his chest. His hair was neat, his cologne the one Riley loved, not his usual one. Greg Robins was clearly out to seduce him that night and Riley was enticed by it.

Greg pulled Riley to him, sliding his free hand into Riley's back pocket, delivering a more romantic kiss that filled Riley's mouth with a flavor of mint and wine. He moved his lips to Riley's neck, tickling and nibbling at him. "Do I need to go visit this Charley guy?" Greg asked, a smile on his face as he moved back to lightly kiss Riley's lips. "Tell him to stop flirting with my man?"

"I'd like that." They had spoke earlier that afternoon about Riley's encounter with the celebrity but he hadn't really gotten the feeling that Greg was affected by what Riley told him. It was nice to know then that Greg had at least paid attention, even if his jealousy hadn't been spoken.

Another light kiss. Greg looked at Riley like he was memorizing his face. "You are so handsome."

"So are you," he smiled, sliding his hand under Greg's shirt to touch his warm skin.

Greg took Riley's glass and set their glasses on the table. He moved back to Riley with his full attention. The kiss was deep and hungry. He held Riley's head to the kiss, his hold tight on him like Riley might get away. "Let's go to bed," Greg said, moving away from the kiss.

Riley knew Greg was moving the night along quickly but he let it happen. He'd like to think more that Greg was just anxious to be with him, not just in a hurry.

The lights were left off as they moved to the guest bedroom. Greg hadn't wanted lights to expose their movement in the house, afraid the neighbors would suspect. Riley never had a problem with it. His desire had been to be with Greg, however that had to be.

The darkness was exciting to him. They were in a basically unfamiliar place, sneaking around, doing sexual things that aroused him to think about. Greg was hiding his life, true, but Riley knew the secret. He knew what it felt like to be made love to by Greg's body, to be held in his strong arms and to hear his vulnerable gasp as he came. They were keeping a secret for Greg's reputation and while it hurt Riley sometimes, it was times like that night that made it all worthwhile.

Greg knew it too, moaning as he ran his hand over Riley's hardening penis. In the darkness, the two faced each other, kissing, removing clothes with a hurried pace, touching and moving towards the bed that knew their secret.

Riley laid over Greg, moving his kisses down Greg's ticklish belly to take him in his mouth. He slid a hand under Greg's butt to massage the best butt he had ever seen. Greg's hands played in Riley's hair. His moans excited Riley even more.

He moved to kiss Greg's lips, making room for him between Greg's legs, barely able to wait to claim Greg's body, but Greg rolled them over really quick.

He moved to quickly bite Riley's neck, nicely hurting him as he moved them. Riley didn't resist, waiting in sweet ecstasy for Greg to take him as they kissed again.

And then the moment Riley loved almost more than his orgasm. Greg was inside him, moving slowly as he got into position and then Riley was completely his, subject to Greg's rhythm and nothing more.

He enjoyed the dark room, keeping his mind focused on Greg's warm body and his groans. It kept out thoughts of Charley having followed him or watching them through the window. Greg had his paranoia and now Riley had his.

The darkness kept him thinking about Greg's penis and the motion and the secret act they did.

The orgasm that rippled through Riley's body seemed to flow into Greg's also and through the room, casting Riley's voice out into the silence. He was only slightly aware that Greg was biting him on the chest, moving against Riley as his body spasmed.

If only the moment could last longer, but it was over, ending with Greg's hungry, almost rough kiss. He moved a few more times inside Riley and then released him, making him moan into Greg's mouth but the kiss was unbroken.

They soon laid side-by-side, exhausted and satisfied. Riley rolled into Greg's arms, rubbing his chest, enjoying the moment after. He lightly kissed Greg's chest, wishing they could go again.

He laid fully on Greg, kissing him slowly and tenderly. He ended the kiss, petting Greg's sweaty hair, looking into the darkness but sure he could see Greg's face. "I love you," he said, unable to say anything more after that night. He lightly kissed Greg's lips and cheeks, knowing he didn't expect Greg to repeat the words but hoping to hear them all the same.

Greg stepped out of the bathroom, letting its light spill into the bedroom. He was dressed after his shower. Riley looked at him, perplexed. He knew their nights there didn't last a long time but they usually had until late at night. Matt worked overnights so it wasn't Matt.

"I've got a lot to do tomorrow. I need to get home early," Greg offered to Riley's unasked question.

"Are we ever going to just spend some time together? Maybe go out somewhere?" He saw those words send fear through Greg. "No," Riley answered his own question. He threw the covers off him with a bit of anger, moving to collect his clothes.

"Don't be mad," Greg said, making Riley feel his anger wasn't warranted and he was being childish.

"Why not? I want to see you for a romantic night and you can't be bothered to spend an hour with me cuddling? Who are you afraid to know you're here? Or are you afraid to know me?"

"I'm not afraid. I'm just busy. I have a life too, Rile."

"That you can't spare me an hour? I drove all this way to see you."

"I'm sorry, Rile. I want to be with you," he said, moving to hug Riley. "Look, we've got that vacation coming up next month. We'll be together then." Greg sealed that promise with a deep kiss. It was a kiss that filled Riley with sadness. That night had been great but in one second, it had been ruined.

He left Greg's hold and gathered up his clothes. He'd go home. He was tired after all.

Tom

Riley had returned home just past midnight. He saw there were three messages on the phone but he chose to ignore them. He went to take a shower and then to bed, letting his body remember its night and not letting his mind analyze it.

He'd slept soundly that night until the phone rang early the next morning. Knowing he had stuff to do, Riley made himself get up and dressed. It was only once breakfast was cooking that he went to his phone to check the messages.

Two were from Charley. He had been the one that called that morning and he called while Riley was replaying the messages. Knowing he'd not get rid of Charley until he talked to him, he answered the phone.

"I was beginning to think you were avoiding me. I thought I'd made you mad."

"No, I just got home late. What can I do for you?"

"Have a good evening with your man?" Charley's voice held an attitude Riley didn't like.

He couldn't bring himself to respond.

"I met someone yesterday," Charley said, as if Riley's answer hadn't been needed. "Very informative source, actually."

Riley sighed, aware Greg's identity had been exposed. "Who was this source?"

"A Rennick Halleran. Quite full of information."

"I bet. Fine, let me have it."

"Seems he doesn't like this guy either."

"He wouldn't know. He's never met him. My father and I aren't exactly close. Did he mention that?"

"No. He did mention he could have you sent to jail real easy, though."

"Yes, because I keep putting my neck out there to cover his crimes and now he gets to take me down with him. He did mention he likes to wreck havoc?"

"What did Greg say about me?" Charley asked as if they spoke of Greg all the time.

He wasn't sure what to say to that. "What was he supposed to say?"

"Just curious," Charley replied with a tone that he knew how the night had ended. "You don't sound good," he continued, sounding honestly concerned.

"I'm tired," Riley lied.

"I'm sorry. You two had a fight, didn't you?"

"Don't worry about it, okay? We fight all the time." The freedom he felt to talk to Charley flared up once again. He quickly worked to stop it. "It wasn't over you so don't get an ego." He sighed, "I've got a lot to do. I'll see you around, okay?"

The call ended leaving Riley feeling worse than he had. It was true, Greg and he did fight a lot. But last night's fight felt different and that troubled him as much as the fight did.

Tom Watts was the man who had been more of a father to Riley. He was an old man but was the only helper Riley had on his farm. With hundreds of acres of hay to make each season, it was overwhelming for him with his regular job and for the 81-year-old man that wouldn't stop working until probably weeks after his body was laid to rest.

It was Tom's arrival that day that finally lifted the funk around him. Tom and Riley got each other, no need to explain actions or defend things. They merely accepted the other because they had a special relationship, a mix of friendship and father/son that was admired by many. They also couldn't keep secrets from each other.

"You look like shit," Tom said, stepping up to Riley's side in the barn later that day.

Tom's old, thin body was supported by a skeleton that had seen wars, picked cotton, farmed hay and cows and had loved Olive Mae for over fifty years. He had a smoker's voice and cough and would have given his shirt for anyone in that town. To most, he was just an old-timer that wasn't worth all that much and had a farm that had seen better days.

To face his old, smiling face, Riley really did feel like shit. He was fifty years younger than Tom but the old man seemed to have more enjoyment in life than Riley ever had. It was something Tom had always possessed. He was jealous of that.

"I had a bad day," Riley smiled, summing it up with that. He didn't mention Greg's name, sure that Tom's opinion of him wasn't much better than Rennick's.

"I met that celebrity the whole town's talking about. Is it a him or a her?" Tom's question was purely naivety talking, not prejudice.

"Don't get started with him. He's part of my bad day."

Tom's smile was telling.

Riley sighed, walking away to the tack room to grab a bridle. "Not you too."

"We didn't talk about you all that much. *He*, is it, seems very interested in you."

"I know that. He's talked to my dad, too. Called me four times to make sure I'm not mad at him."

"He's funny. British, isn't he?"

"When we gonna get started on the hay?" Riley turned the conversation, not wanting to think of Charley or Greg for some time. The stress of planning the hay cutting was overwhelming him. He had two important zoning meetings with the city council coming up as well as a budget to submit and the time off for doing the hay wasn't going to help his bills any. He only hoped to get the hay cut quick and sold even quicker.

"You know," Tom said, leaning against the stable door like a cowboy hanging out at the saloon, "you have such a heaviness around you that it is filling up this barn and possibly the yard outside."

"Thanks. I hadn't noticed."

Tom smiled, showing he was keeping his next statement to himself. After a brief silence, he spoke up, "Is there anything at all I can do to help?"

"Not really. You know you've helped me more than I can ever repay you. I wouldn't dream of asking for anything more."

"I'm offering. Need a hug? A cake? A serenade? What it is?"

It made Riley smile and that had been Tom's intention. "How do I get myself in these messes?"

"You? You jump right in, son. That's how."

Riley nodded. That was accurate. He'd never been passive about anything. "Well, let's get started. We won't get any hay without the tractor running."

The old tractor sat in its regular spot next to the barn where it typically rested between working and broken down. It'd broken down on him mowing one of his smaller fields a few weeks ago. He'd towed it back with the truck and had to wait for a good day to fix it. Riley could do some things but when it came to **broken**, Tom was the mechanical genius. Riley was merely the assistant.

As the heat of the day kicked in and the engine parts began to line the ground around them, Riley heard the sound of an approaching vehicle. Tom actually looked first and let out a cuss that made Riley's heart begin to pound with nerves.

He'd turned, expecting to see the Pacifica's approach but it wasn't that car he saw. It was the Cadillac Escalade belonging to his number one problem: Jonathan Strand.

"What the hell is he doing here?" Tom asked, not bothering to hide his disgust.

"The way my life is going? Probably here to suck out our souls."

The Escalade came to a stop near Tom's beater truck. A man as smooth as the devil and dressed like a slick businessman stepped out. Riley grabbed a towel and tried to wipe the oil off his hands as he walked towards John Strand.

"Hello," Riley said, trying to remain polite. "You're a long way from home." Riley didn't offer his hand to him, knowing he wouldn't have shook it anyway.

"I was just in town looking around. Was in the area and thought you might be available for lunch but you look busy."

"Yeah," he looked back at the tractor reflexively. "Thank you anyway, though."

"Some other time, perhaps. I just wanted to touch base, see if there's anything I can do to help out."

"Nothing, really. Thank you though. The meeting is still on for Tuesday as far as I know," he said, turning the conversation to business.

"Alright," John said, looking around Riley's farm with a smugness. "I will see you then. But I mean it, if there's anything I can do to help out, anything at all, just let me know."

"Thanks. I will."

John left with a nod. Riley watched until the vehicle was headed out the drive and then returned to Tom's side.

"What'd that bastard want?" Tom asked.

"To show off, I think. Perhaps offer a bribe. Anything he can do, just let him know."

"Maybe he wants a date."

Riley laughed. "That jerk?" he smiled, but then after thinking about it, added, "It would fit the pattern, wouldn't it."

Riley's Rough Week

His bad weekend traveled into Monday morning. If he didn't drop something, he spilled it. Even Scarecrow was sassing him that morning. Traffic was horrible and he expected Chief Russell to be waiting to arrest him when he pulled into his parking space.

While Riley wasn't faced with Russell, Lana's expression didn't thrill him all that much.

"I guess you didn't see," she said, a pained wince of concern on her face.

"See what? What happened? The factory didn't back out, did it?"

"No. Worse than that." She handed him the paper turned to the article on Charley Claremont.

His eyes fell right to his name. Reading the paragraph, Charley declared his love for him and offered a vow to romance their lonely mayor. "Oh my…" he choked. He started into his office to make some calls.

"I didn't get to—"

Riley opened the door to find his office filled with roses. Five vases sat on the desk, a vase in every chair and window sill and three on the floor.

"—warn you," Lana finished, stepping in behind him.

"Holy Hell," Riley looked at his office in disbelief. "This has got to stop. He's gonna kill me."

There was no card, no way to reach Charley.

"Get rid of these," Riley told her. "My allergies will kill me."

He left his office, going down the hall to his friend's office. Annette McCellen and he had become friends quickly. She was the accountant for the town, a stern woman with a sense of humor most wouldn't believe. While she didn't smile all that much at work, she looked unusually stressed that day as Riley stepped into her office. She'd seen the article.

"Does everyone know about this but me?" he asked, sitting in the chair opposite her desk. "How could they do this to me, print something like that?"

"I'm sorry. You know we all love you."

"My office is full of flowers! Is he trying to kill me or romance me?"

When Annette took another call, Riley took his cell phone and called Greg. He didn't take Riley's news with quite the same anger.

"Oh my God," Greg gasped, but the slight giggle was in place.

Riley hid his face behind his hand. "I can't take much of this."

"Want me to go beat him up?"

"Actually, yes."

"Would it help?"

Riley thought. "No. I could probably do anything to him and it'd be okay."

"Ah, puppy love."

"Ah, yourself. This is horrible. It's embarrassing."

"It'll pass. If anything, get a restraining order. You're the mayor. Run him out of town. Tar and feathers. Isn't that how it's done?"

Riley wanted to run away.

"Rile? It'll be okay. It'll pass, I promise. Your town knows you. They're enjoying the humor of it and the romance of it. They don't know it bothers you. It'll pass. Your town will still love you."

He sighed, not feeling that positive about it.

"Rile?" Greg said, his tone cautious. "I'm sorry about the other night. I really am. You know how stressed out I get. I didn't mean to hurt you."

That brought a smile to Riley. "Can we get together soon then?"

"I'd like that."

Feeling that the day was taking a turn for the better, Riley walked to the newspaper office on the square, prepared to face Larry Peck, owner of the paper.

"Mayor Halleran," Larry smiled as if he'd been expecting Riley's visit.

"How could you print that? Do you realize the chaos this is causing me?"

"It's news, is all."

"But Larry, come on. This is awful. It's like abuse or something."

"Sorry, Riley, but I have to print what people say. It's character. It's the human interest side that people like."

Riley sighed, "Still, Larry. It's me here. I can't handle this."

"Sorry. We can print a letter or something."

The article was out there, there was no getting that back. And a letter afterwards would only keep it going. Riley gave up. "No. It's done. Just a warning would have been good."

"I'm sorry, Riley. I didn't know it would cause so much trouble for you."

"I know." Riley turned to leave the office, aware his day was going to be full of teases and probably a run-in with Charley Claremont.

Wanting to get the teasing over with was the only reason he stepped foot in the café that afternoon for lunch. The regulars were there with their expected teases.

"Well, if it isn't Mr. Claremont," one said.

"Mr. Mayor, if you were lonely," Clara the waitress started, "you coulda called me anytime."

"So when's the wedding?" Bill asked, laughing a bit too much for Riley's comfort.

"Fine, fine. Get it all out."

The jokes continues, blending together in his mind. Riley hoped to forget them all or he might find himself mad at these people for a long time.

Perhaps they saw how it was bothering him, or they simply ran out of jokes, but they fell back into regular conversations and although he ate quietly, Riley felt like he was still a part of their group.

Returning back to his office, his cell phone rang. He answered out of habit, not looking to see who it was.

"I felt I needed to call to explain."

Charley's voice was innocent of the disaster of his morning.

"Now you have my cell number?" he asked in reflex.

"Riley, I simply said things. You know how I am. I'm boisterous. I said stuff."

"What about the flowers?"

"Well," Charley paused, "that might have been honest."

"I'm allergic to flowers. I haven't been in my office all day."

"Oh. I wondered why you hadn't called."

"I don't have your numbers like you have all of mine."

"I'm sorry. I just thought…" he stopped his sentence, Mr. Talkative suddenly quiet.

"I should appreciate the gesture and I'm sorry but this is only making me uncomfortable."

"Understood. I will slow down the romance then."

"No. There is no romance."

"Humph," Charley said, then adopted a new tone. "I like hard-to-get," he said then ended his call.

"Great" Riley sighed, slamming his phone shut.

Tuesday didn't start out any better and ended with the city council meeting that was going to allow John Strand to submit his request for the land off Highway B to be rezoned from farm land to allow the subdivision he wanted. He was also in the running for buying out ole lady Kelley's farm when it went into default later that month. That would make way for his subdivisions to occupy more of the town's limits than farm land.

It was a prospect that settled horribly in Riley. It was true the town was dying financially. It worried Riley that the council might vote to pass Strand's request only because he promised financial gain for the community as well.

The formal proceedings of the meeting went quickly and smooth, despite Riley's uneasiness. John Strand sat amongst the small gathering with one man who must have been his lawyer and another that could have been his financial advisor. Riley felt outnumbered.

And when his father walked in, he felt sunk. He felt the night was going to end with his town destroyed and himself sitting in jail after his father caused a scene.

Riley had the members of the council sitting around him, but John Strand looked only at him, spoke only to him. That meeting was going to be a battle between Strand and himself.

Strand spoke of the money to be gained, the new housing for a financially strapped community, the draw of new people and community to the town. He laid out the plan for his subdivision and showed drawings of what was to be, a promise of nothing less than Utopia.

Riley politely listened, resisted the urge to fall under Strand's spell and then thanked him nicely for his presentation. The council would take it under advisement and issue a decision at the next meeting three weeks later.

Then Rennick Halleran asked to speak. With no valid reason to deny him, Riley waited anxiously as his father moved to the podium. Rennick spoke of the cheapness of the homes, of how the value of the neighborhoods fell rapidly once they were completed and had photographic evidence of the general failure of the homes ten years down the road as the cheap materials began to rot.

Riley hadn't always agreed with his father but that night, they were in that defense together. He offered his dad the same polite parting, hoping he wasn't acknowledging his father different than he would anyone else. The meeting ended after that with the promise of meeting again in three weeks formally and they left the council chamber to meet privately.

The group was quiet, knowing Riley's dislike of the subdivision to begin with. If any of them were for it, they would have resisted saying so that night. Most of them, much to Riley's hope, seemed to honestly be against the subdivision and rezoning. Like Riley, most of the members had grown up in that town and they wanted to preserve it.

Wednesday afternoon had Riley driving to Midland and to the state auditor's office to sign release forms for them to audit Sleeper. It was an irritation that didn't surprise him too much with the way things were going for him. Although he knew the books were clean and trusted all the employees, it didn't stop Riley's concern that something fraudulent would be found and he'd be defending that accusation as well as the subdivision and the town's failing budget and whatever new challenges came his way as he seemed to be attracting only troubles.

He signed the forms, listened to the speech of how it was a routine audit but he felt like a criminal they were out to get and couldn't help but think Strand had arranged this little part of the game.

It was only stepping outside and planning to head home that a brief wind of happiness hit him. Across the street from the City Hall was a gathering of people standing around a cameraman and reporter, watching as the handsome man reported on the story. Riley walked to his truck and then leaned against the back bumper, watching the scene himself.

Greg was the reporter and he looked gorgeous, a degree of a shine about him as he was in his element, doing the job he loved to do. Riley couldn't hear the words but every so often Greg would point back at the restaurant they stood in front of. He held a notebook in his hand but he never referred to it. He was perfect at his job, knowing his facts and what he intended to say with no misspoken words or stalls. As a public speaker, Greg was one of the best. Riley admired that about him and had to admit he was a bit jealous. He was a public speaker only by necessity. Greg was a natural.

Riley watched the scene feeling like the proud husband. That was his man out there, his gorgeous man that was getting the attention of the ladies that would never have him.

And then the moment that made Riley's heart trip over itself. Greg had stopped talking, taking a break to adjust the tie he wore (and hated), and had glanced out over the crowd. His eyes had passed by Riley and then quickly back to him. There had been a quick moment of him recognizing Riley was there and then the sweetest smile spread across his face and Riley felt himself falling in love all over again. Greg didn't offer a wave, just that smile.

Greg's perfect performance that had been just moments before was suddenly distracted and uncomfortable. Riley found it humorous that he had affected his lover like that.

He thought about leaving, letting Greg get back to *his* world and be Greg Robbins but he wasn't sure leaving was the right thing to do either. He didn't feel right about leaving without speaking to him.

It occurred to him then that Greg might not want him to come over there. That thought hurt him as much as the smile had made him want to fly.

He decided then to leave. Greg wouldn't have wanted him to interfere. He'd forgotten who he was, he told himself as he moved to sit behind the wheel. He was the mistress, not the wife. He wasn't even a buddy whom Greg would want to high-five.

Riley started the engine, feeling all the heaviness return to him of why he was there and a new layer added of being unwanted in his lover's life.

Looking in the mirror to back out of the parking space, Riley saw Greg running across the road though, headed towards him. It made him smile but it didn't replace the joy that had first been there. He put the truck in park and waited.

Greg came to the passenger's window. Riley rolled it down, feeling a bit angry that he hadn't come to the driver's window. "You're a surprise."

"So are you. I just had to come sign some papers. The town's being audited."

"Yikes," Greg winced and made Riley feel better with his show of empathy at least. "Something wrong?"

"Not that I know of. Just one more pain in my ass," he said with a bit too much emotion but Greg didn't pick up on it. How would he know that he was adding to the list of irritations, Riley thought, getting a bit more upset. "What are you doing?"

"Oh, just working," Greg looked back at the spot where he'd been. "The city wants to tear the place down and the people don't want them to. Standard troubles." Greg looked back at him, not meeting his eyes though. "It was a nice surprise to see you though."

Riley smiled. "You looked good out there. I was proud."

"Thanks," Greg smiled, a bit of blush to his face. "I wish we could go to lunch or something."

Or something. "Me, too."

"I've got to get back to work though. Maybe I'll see you soon?"

"I'd like that," he smiled, wanting to add that he was there anytime Greg was ready but it only made him feel bad.

Greg stepped back from the truck, smiling at him. "I'll see you then."

"Bye." He watched Greg leave the lot and run back across the street. He backed out and prepared to head for home. He didn't look again to see what Greg was doing, if he was watching, because he knew he'd catch Greg working and not watching him and it would only make him more angry so he just drove on.

"I'm not gay," Greg had said after their first kiss. Riley remember his slight panic as if it had just happened. They had shared dinner at Riley's house and their bodies just seemed drawn together. They had slow danced in the living room, quickly moving to that first kiss. Greg's words after the kiss had made Riley think he'd misread the whole situation. He guessed Greg hadn't been flirting with him the day they had met. There hadn't really been the stolen glances and sweet smiles shared. It hadn't been a romantic night that Greg had come over for.

Before he could apologize and move away, Greg continued his thought, perhaps seeing he had troubled Riley. "I've never been with a man although I've always been attracted to them. I want to be honest with you. You seem very trustworthy and genuine and I don't want to hurt that."

"You can trust me," Riley had said, petting Greg's cheek and sliding his fingers into Greg's hair.

"I have a wife," Greg said, looking at their shoes but still holding Riley close to him. "I have lived the life my parent's expected of me. Went to the right school, got the great job, the pretty wife, the nice house. But it's not who I am," Greg's eyes were full of sadness as he met Riley's eyes then. "I was pretending to be that man and then I met you and I realized I was lying to everyone, myself included. I can't lie to you."

He didn't want to soil his reputation with his family or the people of the city that watched him on the news every weeknight. There couldn't be rumors. There couldn't be any trouble. If Riley could accept that, he'd like to see him. If not, then perhaps he'd better go home. He would work on getting to be the man he wanted to be, but he needed time. He would step out of that lie he was living. He just had to find the bravery to do so.

But that had been two years ago and Greg was still living in that life and Riley was still giving him time to find his strength. He knew Greg's family was involved in Greg's life. He couldn't be sure but he thought the parents lived on the same road as Greg and the little wife. No doubt they were over every morning for coffee and gossip.

Riley drove home with thoughts of their past turning over in his mind and still fighting the anger that had come to him just as quick as the admiration had. He searched for the right words to sum up what he was feeling then. He tried to recapture the proud feeling of watching Greg. Tried to get the love that swelled with that moment to remain but it faded into anger.

And after his hour drive home and thinking and questioning everything about his and Greg's relationship, the best he could describe his feelings was that he was lonely. He didn't want to be the mistress anymore, never really had wanted to be. He wanted a husband. He wanted to look in the passenger's seat and see that man there with him.

All he felt that day was an empty place in life where his husband was supposed to be.

That thought only brought with it more sadness because he knew when he discussed their future with Greg he was only going to get his heart broke.

Greg's Surprise

By Thursday, Riley was starting to think his week might turn out okay, but the simple act of returning from lunch became something more.

Walking out of the café, he saw Charley walking in a quick pace towards him.

"Oh, no," Riley sighed, watching the man's graceful steps across the street.

"Mr. Mayor," he said, stopping at Riley's side. "I want you to read this introduction I did for you. See if you like it. I swear, you've got to be on my show. The world will love you."

"I don't want to—"

"—Just read it. See what you think. Let me know. Thank you, dear," he said, blew Riley a kiss and was off down the sidewalk with energy aboard.

Riley looked at the couple passing, aware that had all been witnessed. "Good afternoon," he smiled, his tone hiding a bit of the irritation he felt at their stares. He just meant to call them on their watching him.

They replied nicely back and moved on. Riley looked away from their knowing smiles. Was his town turning on him too?

He left the office late Friday night, tired. The day had been full of people and phone calls and the marching band going around the square for two solid hours until the police finally got them to stop.

He hadn't planned on such a busy day, but it hadn't surprised him. His week had been rough on him, out of the norm and exhausting. There was no doubt a full moon in the sky behind the storm clouds bringing forth all the chaos. Riley had stopped trying to control it or change it and just merely tried to go with it and get through.

But the week was over. He'd made it through a day of not hearing from Charley, John Strand or Rennick. As tired as he was, Riley considered it a good day.

Pulling into his drive, he spotted Greg's car and all the troubles about him washed away. Greg had surprised him and he was going to believe it was for a good reason.

Inside, Greg met him at the door with a glass of wine. The smell of dinner cooking floated through the house. Candles were lit and nice music played softly in the background.

"I could get used to this," Riley said as he accepted the wine glass.

Greg smiled, saying nothing, just offered him a light kiss.

Peeking under the skillet's lid, Riley surveyed dinner. "I'm starving suddenly."

"I thought you would be. I wanted to surprise you."

"I like it. You coulda warned me though. I'd have cleaned house a bit."

"Nonsense," Greg said, standing before Riley and sliding his hand into Riley's back pocket. "That would have taken the surprise out of it. And it looks fine." Greg moved in front of Riley, gently moving him back to rest against the cabinet and setting his glass down. "Besides," he said moving in close to Riley's lips, "I don't come here to look at your house."

The kiss was deep, Greg's tongue exploring Riley's mouth. He held Riley tightly to him, unforgiving in his kiss. They broke only when the stove's timer sounded. Greg smiled devilishly at him. "You'll have to wait until after dinner for dessert."

Their mood calmed a bit as their focus turned to food. Their conversation turned to their day. Greg's consisted of dealing with his rotten producer and griping about a CEO of the local hospital he'd really like to take down but the station wouldn't let him do an exposé on. Riley's concerns were as bothersome, Strand and the zoning fight and the never-ending parade of people coming to his office expecting him to be judge in their troubles. He didn't mention Charley's name at all. Didn't even want to think about Charley.

After they'd eaten and talked some more, Riley started collecting the dishes and took them to the kitchen. Greg followed and slid his arms around Riley's waist. "Leave them," he whispered, grinding his hips against Riley. "This can wait. I'll do them tomorrow."

"Tomorrow?" Riley asked, not trying to be mean with his question but worried Greg would have taken it that way.

"Yes. Tomorrow," Greg whispered into his ear. "I'm staying until Sunday, if that's okay with you."

"Okay?" he smiled, feeling a rush of happiness. "You know I'd love that."

"That's why I'm here," Greg said, then kissed Riley's neck. "So leave the dishes. Although," he slid his hand over the front of

Riley's jeans, "I do like this." He slid one hand under Riley's shirt and moved the other hand between Riley's legs and held him.

Riley closed his eyes, bracing himself against the cabinet and enjoying Greg's hands searching his body. Greg lifted Riley's shirt and pulled it off then returned to touching him. His warm lips moved over Riley's back.

Turning in Greg's arms, he held Greg's head and deeply kissed his lips. Their tongues paired and danced as their bodies tried to move as close together as they could.

Greg tried to undo Riley's jeans with one hand and such urgency it made Riley giggle. Greg smiled, giving up on the kissing and undressing and moved to undo and remove Riley's jeans and then his own before returning to kiss him.

Greg's kiss was urgent, his tongue exploring deeply and his hold on Riley strong. His hand was searching Riley's body as urgently as the kiss. As Riley's hands moved Greg's underwear down and then went to the erection there, Greg moaned into his mouth then moved back. He took Riley's hand and led him into the bedroom.

Greg left the light off but there was enough light outside for them to see. At the side of the bed, Greg removed Riley's briefs and then kissed him again.

Riley met every kiss, every touch, echoing the hunger of Greg. He let Greg sit him on the bed, waiting as Greg fumbled with the lube and condom. Teasingly, he bit Greg's leg as he waited, touching all he could.

Ready, Greg tossed him back to the bed. Riley closed his eyes, willing to let Greg control him, the gentle master he knew. He felt his legs be lifted, desperate for the sweet moment he craved and feared at the same time. Penetration was his favorite part and Greg knew it, teasing him, making him wait for it.

Lifted up slightly from the bed, Riley felt Greg's hard thickness ease inside him. Greg was gentle but strong with him, ensuring he was comfortable before Greg gave into his desire and quickened his pace.

Riley didn't care what Greg did to him. He loved every action. He loved the sound of their bodies hitting. He loved the feel of his body being rocked, being taken. He loved the awkward position of his body and the private act they were doing. He loved the feel of Greg inside him most of all and the feel of Greg's hands holding him.

Greg's rhythm was rigid and quick. Riley knew he would be coming soon. Losing himself in the darkness of the room and the secretiveness of their lovemaking, Riley gave himself over to the feel of his body's being made love to and let himself go. He felt Greg's body spasm against his and heard Greg's groans but it was in his own breath-taking spasm that he stayed and listened to his groan and felt his body ease down as the moment hit and passed.

Greg thrust deep once more, making Riley tense with the action. He laid still as Greg withdrew and released his leg. Greg moved to lay over him, kissing him sweetly, breathing heavy from his experience but tending to Riley.

Riley kissed him, holding his lover to him, entangling their legs that hung over the side of the bed. He closed his eyes, letting Greg move from his lips to kiss his neck and chest, enjoying the slow wave of passion still about them. He slid his fingers through Greg's hair, meaning to pull him back to his kiss when Greg stopped just at the edge of Riley's kiss.

"I love you," Greg said.

Riley was sure his heart had stopped, despite its rapid pace. He smiled, pulling Greg to a kiss that was much more than he'd first thought it would be.

Too tired to kiss anymore, Riley held Greg's body tightly, feeling as if their hold was for the first time unified. "I love you, too."

Weekend with Greg

The sun was shining brightly when Riley woke. He didn't care what time it was, just that when he opened his eyes, Greg's side was empty. *He didn't stay.*

But then he heard a sound in the hallway. Looking towards the door, Riley smiled to see Greg enter the room. He wore Riley's robe and carried two coffee cups.

"You are here."

"I said I'd stay," Greg smiled, sitting beside Riley. "I'm fixing breakfast. Should be ready by the time you get up."

Riley got a glimpse of the clock, finding it was after ten. "Why'd you let me sleep all morning?"

"Because I know you needed your rest," Greg said, moving in to kiss Riley's lips, smiling slyly at him. "And because I know you'll need your rest for this evening as well."

He smiled back at his lover, getting lost in Greg's eyes for a moment. He was sore when he stood up and it made him feel good. He liked that kind of soreness, knowing his body had had the perfect workout the night before. Greg found it humorous.

"What's your plan for today?" Riley asked as they sat at breakfast.

"I thought maybe we'd go eat lunch somewhere. I thought about going to look at Jonathon Strand's subdivision going up near the city. I'd like to do a piece on him, expose his lies."

"I wish you would. I feel like the only person out here fighting him. It'd be great if you'd take him down before I had to deal with him."

"I'd love to. The station won't let me touch him though."

"Why not? He's obviously doing something crooked."

"He has money. They don't like to touch people with clout."

"Isn't that the job, though? Show the truth in the news?"

Greg shrugged. "I don't think so."

"Why don't you do a story anyway? Become the voice of the people?"

"You know me, Rile. I have big dreams but I couldn't stand up against these guys. They'd tear me apart."

Riley saw the sadness flow over Greg's expression. The insecurity Greg had lived with and excepted in himself controlled him. "You could try. The only failure is not trying."

"I'm not like you, Rie. I'm more bubble-gum," he smiled, but Riley felt the smile was covering the anger he felt at himself. "I should have been a weather man or, I don't know, the adopt-this-dog reporter."

He wasn't sure what Greg wanted to hear so he remained quiet.

Greg continued, "I'm not all strong and politically-opinionated and so sure that I'm right. You run this town, you know that? You got the big factory in here. You kept the big chains out. The town depends on you to decide what to wear today."

"I just do what I have to. Trust me, sometimes I wish I could just care about my hay fields and not what the town needs to do. But I care about this town. It's my home. I care about you. I want to help you however I can."

Greg smiled at him, letting some of his fret ease. "You do. You're my inspiration."

Riley laughed. "You're just being cheesy now. I'm serious. Whatever pep talk it is you need, I'm here."

Greg nodded, looking at his fork as he moved his cold breakfast around on the plate. "Just let me hide here with you. I feel right around you. I feel like the world is a good place around you, here."

He reached over and held Greg's hand. Riley was beginning to understand the depth of Greg's unhappiness of his other world and yet he lacked the strength to leave it. "Let's enjoy today then. Perhaps you'll feel better. You don't worry. I won't worry about anything in my life. We'll just have fun for a change. We'll go look at the houses and see what we find." Riley didn't speak his next thought, but he hoped that looking at the houses would inspire Greg to do the report on Strand and bring the land tycoon down and lift Greg into the career he wanted and solve two of Riley's problems at the same time: the subdivision zoning and Greg's depression.

The subdivision was what Riley had expected. The houses were close together with barely room to mow the yard between them. They were all the same design, vinyl siding and shutters that looked cheap and in awful colors. There were virtually no trees or landscaping.

Riley felt claustrophobic as Greg drove down another street of the same. He could only shake his head as house after house passed him by. "These are awful," he sighed.

"The payments are cheap is what gets people in," Greg reported as he turned onto another street. "Strand offers 10-year loans with a balloon payment at the end. Trouble is, his houses don't hold their value so people end up stuck with a huge loan they can't pay. He repos the house, sells it again. Or, like this neighborhood, you have a lot of empty houses just taking up space."

"Someone has to stop him. He's preying on my town because he knows he has us. The money from the sell of the land would float us for twenty years." Riley shook his head again, feeling his heart sink that he had to vote against that part of it. The town was going broke, he couldn't argue that. He'd managed to keep them going for a while, but how long before some new disaster happened. He'd been lucky with the factory deal. He might not have any luck left.

But to vote for Strand just because they needed the money? It didn't feel right. The idea that all that beautiful farmland would be destroyed for a scenery of this mess just made Riley ill.

Then one house at the end of the street caught their attention. Greg slowed down, moving to the curb so they could get an uninterrupted look. Spray paint covered the garage door and front of the house. Things like "Go Away Strand" and "My house sucks!" were painted over windows and siding.

"That looks like something my dad would do," Riley noted.

The neighboring house had "Cheap Homes. Stay Away!" down the side and "Beware" across the garage door.

"Wow," Greg sighed, "Someone's not happy."

"See? Your piece would have an audience," Riley said, meaning to encourage Greg. "You've done your homework on the man obviously. Let people know how awful this is. I'll stand with you." He looked back at the houses, "These people will stand with you."

Greg nodded but said nothing.

Riley didn't press him. He looked back at the houses knowing that despite whatever financial ruin waited for the town and himself, he could not allow these houses anywhere near.

It wasn't like Riley and Greg had never eaten out before. They had just never eaten out in a place where Greg might have been recognized. Even as they ate at McDonald's that afternoon, Greg looked anxious and uncomfortable. He kept his head down or looked to the left if someone passed on his right. Riley felt pressured to eat quickly just so they could leave.

It was finally too much for him. "Do we need to go?" Riley asked, trying to keep his irritation at Greg's behavior hidden.

"No," was Greg's response but Riley knew it was lie.

"We're just eating lunch," he whispered.

But then it hit him why Greg was so uneasy.

He began gathering up his food. "We can eat on the road," he said. "That's fine."

"No," Greg spoke up. "We'll stay," he offered, like he meant to be brave or that perhaps Riley had the wrong idea about why he was acting that way.

"I'm done. Let's go." Riley stood up, knowing that Greg would follow, not about to make a scene in a public place when he didn't even want to be seen sitting with a gay man.

Riley threw his stuff away, no longer hungry. In silence, they walked to Greg's car and rode some distance before Greg's phone rang. He answered it in a happy tone, like there wasn't an upset male lover sitting next to him.

It was clearly Greg's wife on the phone. Riley blocked the moment from his mind as a Greg he didn't know appeared in the car. His tone and mood changed drastically, turning him into some false pretense of a person Riley loved.

He chose instead to look out the window and let himself be consumed with the disappointment of a man beside him, the pressure of having to fight the subdivision and the stress of his failing farm. He closed his eyes and wished his life could be totally different as Dolly sang on the radio *"What a heartache you turned out to be..."*

By the time they reached the house, Riley was feeling bad about being angry at Greg. He didn't want them to fight. Greg's silence was making him feel as if he were to blame for that awful afternoon. He wanted the day to go back to the two of them being together. There was so much inside him that he wanted to say, he just didn't want to fight. He needed one thing in his life to be stress free. Why couldn't Greg be that one thing?

Inside the house he let the pouting silence continue. He saw there were four messages on his phone but he didn't check them. He went to the kitchen and started fixing himself something to drink, hoping that Greg didn't go into the bedroom and start packing his stuff.

But Greg stopped in the entryway of the kitchen and looked at his shoes like a sorrowful boy.

"Do you want something to drink?" Riley asked plainly, no anger but no forgiveness in his tone.

"No."

Riley forced himself to be quiet. He was curious what Greg would do.

"I'm sorry for that back there," Greg finally said, his words spoken softly.

"For which part?" The question seemed to surprise and confuse Greg. "For the restaurant or for the car ride?" he added, clarifying it for him.

"It stresses me out. I'm afraid someone will notice me and…" he stopped.

"And ask who I am?" Riley looked him in the eyes, daring him to deny that.

"I don't know what I would say."

"Say "your friend Riley." That's all they need to know. Two guys can go out and eat together. That doesn't mean a thing."

Greg was quiet, like he was gathering the courage to say what he really felt.

"Because of me?" Riley asked him. "Because someone might know who I am and know that I'm gay? So what? That doesn't mean anything about you. People will think whatever they want no matter what you tell them or prove to them. Someone might think you're gay even though you have a wife. You can't stop that."

"I know. It's just hard for me to get comfortable. I've been scared for so many years of who I am."

"Fine. We won't go out and eat ever again. Or we'll sit at different tables maybe. Whatever."

Greg smiled but he didn't offer any resistance to Riley's plan. He stepped in closer to Riley, but still avoided eye contact. "I am sorry about the phone call too. I have to be two different people. I'm like an actor."

"With which one of us?"

"Not with you. I feel right around you."

"Then why don't you stay? You don't have to be that other person."

That made Greg retreat back to his shell. "I'm not ready," he said. "It would destroy my family, my wife, my career."

"Then I'd say you don't really feel right around me." He said the words even though he feared what reaction they would bring. "You'd lose all that important stuff if you chose me. So you choose all that important stuff and you only lose me. Isn't that what you're saying?" he looked at Greg and saw a hint of anger at the truth in his eyes and also a sadness of his heart breaking.

"It's complicated, Rie," he finally said, his voice wavering like he was about to cry. "I'm not strong like you are. I'm trying to be, though. I need time."

Riley closed his eyes, letting out a slow breath. He'd known that about Greg when he'd met him. Greg's religious upbringing had caused such a riff in his life that Greg had almost been lost when they'd met. He'd been so unhappy and burdened with his feelings he knew to be right for him when the world (his family) had told him how wrong it had been.

Greg had said from the beginning that he would have to hide and would need time to get strong enough for the transition from the old Greg to the new Greg he wanted to be. Riley had known this and had accepted the relationship and he felt wrong that day to expect more from his lover. Greg needed time so Riley backed down from his argument.

"It just hurts," he said.

"I know," Greg said, moving in and holding him. "I know," he whispered into Riley's ear. "I am sorry." He lightly kissed Riley's cheek then hugged him, squeezing him tight. "I'm sorry."

Riley remained in the hold, closing his eyes. He squeezed Greg's strong body, needing to remember what it felt like to be held. "I need more," he said, feeling a fear move through him as he said the words.

Greg slowly moved back from the hold but his gaze was on their shoes. "What do you mean?"

"I mean I'm tired of this for us. Why can't we just be together? No one will care, Greg, really. So the news guy is gay. So what?"

Greg looked away, getting that angry expression that Riley honestly feared.

"I'm just saying that I love you and when I saw you the other day I was so happy because I knew that was my man out there. But, that's not true," he said then paused. "I just want us to be together. I don't want to be the other lover."

"I know you don't." Greg licked his lips, looking nervously away as he tried to say something more but the words didn't come.

"When is that going to happen? Is it?"

"Yes," Greg looked at him then but his response lacked strength. "Yes, I want to be with you. I'm just…," he said then stopped as if searching for the right word. "I'm just trapped."

"You're not trapped. Trapped in what? Marriage?"

"I don't want to hurt her."

"So you hurt me instead."

"No. I don't want to hurt you either," Greg said, a look of true concern in his eyes. He reached out and petted Riley's arms. "I don't want us to be this complicated. We just are."

"We don't have to be. We can be together."

Greg looked down, making Riley's argument for their relationship stall. He'd hoped for the immediate pledge of love from Greg but had expected the battle they were starting then.

Greg wouldn't commit to him, only to the sometime relationship they had.

Riley sighed, a part of him wanting to undo his words and just let them continue with their cheating relationship and he would just take all his loneliness and anger and bury it away and just enjoy the sex.

Greg stepped up to him and slid his hands around Riley's body and he knew he would do whatever Greg wanted. The man before him was addictive and Riley couldn't fight it. Greg knew what to do, knew how to keep him hooked. His kisses knew the right spots on Riley's neck and chest. His hands knew just how to slide into Riley's jeans and awaken him and put out any thoughts of talking.

His lover unzipped his jeans and pulled them down as his kisses moved down Riley's chest. There was a want to stop what was happening because he wanted to hear the words from Greg that he was sorry but Riley's voice didn't utter Greg's name loud enough to stop what Greg was doing to him.

It was only once Riley's body was fully awake and hungry for more that Greg left him and stood. Greg cupped Riley's face in his hands and pulled him to a kiss and to his tongue that explored Riley's mouth urgently.

The kiss stopped and their eyes met and locked. Greg studied him for what seemed to be the longest time. Riley denied himself to see the sadness in Greg's eyes.

"Let's go to bed," Greg said.

It was his belief that Greg never let Riley make love to him because that would confirm Greg was gay. Greg was always the one on top. Riley didn't mind. He liked Greg making love to him. But there was just that suspicion in Riley's mind that Greg refused him because he would still be a straight man that way.

Flawed thinking, sure, but it seemed logical in Greg's thinking.

Riley expected nothing different that night as they laid in bed. The night was like all others: lights out, music playing, Greg laying on him, leading the night. But the unwanted feeling hit Riley when Greg raised up and looked at him. There was just enough light for Riley to know Greg was looking at him, but Greg's expression was shaded. Greg resisted his kisses, remaining over him like he was studying Riley or perhaps preparing a speech.

And that thought scared Riley. His heart filled with pain as he was sure this was their last night together. Greg was trying to form the words to break up with him. He was about to admit that he couldn't be two different people and Riley was right about him. He was going to choose those important things and lose Riley.

The silence was too much for Riley. There were too many suspected thoughts going through his mind that he thought were going through Greg's. And Greg was offering nothing.

"What?" Riley finally asked, concerned.

Greg moved back a bit, trying to speak a few times but then giving up, like words were failing him.

Riley felt like he was at the moment of their breakup and feared he was going to cry. He pulled his arm back, letting Greg go, thinking his touch wasn't wanted.

Greg grabbed his hand and held it. "I wish I was you."

"Why?"

"You're so strong and unafraid."

"That's not true," he said, thinking that the next few minutes were going to prove how wrong Greg's words were. He was so afraid Greg was leaving him and any ounce of strength was going to be washed away in his unhappiness.

Greg leaned down and nibbled on Riley's ear and then whispered his thought.

Riley smiled at all his wrong thoughts. It hadn't been the end of their relationship brewing, it had been a new beginning.

Riley controlled the kisses and the touches. As he positioned himself behind Greg, he felt Greg's body tremble. Greg raised up and braced himself against the headboard as Riley gently entered him. Riley had never heard Greg cuss, but at that moment the sweetest little curse word came from his mouth.

He moved delicately and tenderly as Greg's body gave way to him, enjoying the mere fact that Greg had given himself to him. Words of love spoken the night before and now Riley was inside him, owning him.

He felt his life was changing for the better after all. Greg was finding the strength he needed to become that awesome reporter and Riley's husband. The future was there, Riley thought, and it had started with lovemaking.

A Clown's Birthday Party

Riley walked with Greg to his car late that Sunday morning. They walked with their arms around the other, bodies close but very little words said. For Riley, it was an awkward moment approaching and he wasn't sure why he felt that way.

He enjoyed the fact that Greg was a little sore that morning after their night. Greg offered him kisses and promises of plans for the vacation they had scheduled soon. The idea of the two of them alone in another state where there were no inhibitions or insecurities brought his body to life again with fantasies of wild nights to be.

He let Greg go long enough for the bag to be tossed into the backseat then Greg returned to face him. Greg's hands went into his pockets, like he no longer wanted contact with his male lover in the presence of the car or the world beyond the house.

"I wish you'd come to this thing today," Riley said, having asked Greg to be at his side already and getting shot down. "I'd like to see you in the audience."

Greg smiled, his polite way of telling Riley not to start that talk again.

He merely nodded. "Well, call me. Can I have a kiss?"

"Sure." Greg leaned in and gave him a tender kiss, one more daring than Riley had expected. "I'll see you later."

"Later."

Riley stepped back and watched Greg get in his fancy car and drive away. He knew Greg would stop at the car wash and wash away all traces of the dirt road and then would probably go home and shower and wash away any traces of Riley.

But he stopped that line of thought, simply waved once again as Greg drove away, and made himself remember that Greg had told him he'd loved him and forced his weird feelings to stay away.

Heading into town later that afternoon, Riley battled his usual round of nerves. He hated giving speeches even though once he was on stage he felt fine. With some time to wait before he was needed in the town square, he decided to go to the café, and attempt to eat something and perhaps write his speech for that day.

But as he stepped inside, his attention immediately fell on Charley Claremont.

It was too late to turn around so he moved into the diner and to a booth at the back. Charley sat at a small table near the front, a cup of coffee before him and a wrapped present sitting beside him. He was on a cell phone, speaking French and laughing a lot. Riley tried to sneak past the table like a sheep tiptoeing past a wolf.

He sat with his back to Charley, smiling as the waitress came to take his order. After she left, he had nothing to do but stare out the window and listen to Charley's animated conversation. His appetite was going away the more he dreaded Charley coming over, which he knew would happen.

It was less than a minute after the phone call ended that he heard the rustle of the package and footsteps towards him and then Charley was sitting across him in the booth. The package was handed over.

"I made this for you," he nodded. He folded his hands under his chin as he waited for Riley to open it. His nails were a bright red that matched his lipstick. His make-up was less dramatic that day as was his hair. He wore a seventies-colored tight shirt and a few bracelets and two watches. His smile was genuine.

"Go on," he continued. "Open it."

Riley looked nervously around the café, finding the waitress was watching them, as if watching her favorite soap opera. "Charley, please."

"What? Am I making a spectacle? I simply made you something. Do I embarrass you?" he asked, smiling, as if he knew the answer and thrived on people's discomfort.

"Yes," Riley replied, keeping his voice low.

"Well, open the ding-dong box and then I'll go away," Charley dared.

Riley sighed, taking the box and removing the paper.

"Be careful with it. It's breakable."

Praying that it wasn't something sexual or horribly embarrassing, he removed the top of the box to find a statue nestled in white tissue paper. Upon first sight of it his worry was removed.

He lifted it out carefully, finding himself speechless. Standing before him was the image of a man's turned down head, nestled against the nose of a horse whose head rested on the man's shoulder. The man's hand was resting on the other side of the horse's muzzle. It could have very well been himself and Scarecrow.

"Wow," was all he could find to say, unable to look at Charley.

"I made it for you. Couldn't help myself. It's a translation of your aura."

Riley smiled at him, "Thank you. It's wonderful."

Everyone knew he had horses but no one knew his *love* for them. Charley had been the first to pick up on it.

The waitress came over with his food. "That's awesome!" she said, leaning in to look at it. "You did that?" she asked Charley.

"I did. Thanks."

Riley listened as the waitress and Charley exchanged their fan/celebrity banter, her full of compliments and big fan and he with the thanks-so-much, that-means-a-lot, but Riley's attention was on the sculpture and he felt awful that Charley had done something so wonderful for him and he'd not even tried to be nice to the celebrity before him.

"Any-way," Charley said, his eyes getting wide as he smiled at Riley. "I should go. Just wanted to give you that. You have a great day. Good luck with the speech and all," he continued as he stood.

"You don't have to run off," Riley heard himself saying, curious about Charley's talent and ability to pick up on his aura.

"Got stuff to do," Charley said, wrinkling his nose as he let his persona Charley speak. "But I'll see you at the gig today. Should be fun," he said, gently touching Riley's shoulder as he moved on.

"Well, thanks very much for this," Riley said, turning to watch him walk away. "It's great."

Charley smiled at him, nodding, and in his signature flare, Charley had said farewells to those there, collected his bag and phone, left a tip and was out the door.

He looked back at his gift, not able to hold in his smile or ignore the look that was in Charley's eyes, a longing and sadness that filled him as he looked upon Riley.

Riley ate his lunch, aware he was filled with a giddiness he was becoming comfortable with and didn't even think about being nervous about his speech. It had been a long time, if ever, that someone had flirted with him or tried to romance him. Greg's romance of him hadn't been that involved really. Riley had done more of the romancing and they'd just gotten together. This was a new experience and he was liking it.

He carefully repacked the statue and went to pay for his lunch, where he was told that Ms. Claremont had already paid for his.

Riley left the café, with a smile on his face that he couldn't shake.

Ed Seigler had been born and raised in Sleeper. Legend had him as class clown to football hero. What was true was Ed had gone on to fame as Pappy, the sad rodeo clown. Fame, in that twenty years after his death, his character and image were still sold and the town still celebrated his birthday every year.

It was to that ceremony Riley walked to. His main function was to introduce the speakers and keep the program going so he wasn't as nervous as some of his past speeches. But he also had other things on his mind, like being flirted with by a good-looking man and wondering if Greg would be jealous.

So it was with that distant attention that he thought he'd seen Charley step out from the corner of a building and then quickly back when he'd spotted Riley. Having not really been paying attention, he wrote it off to his active mind and went on.

Perhaps Charley had just been following him, if he'd really been there. Scott Duver was waving him over to the square's gazebo so he didn't bother to investigate.

The ceremony would consist of memories of Ed, great stories of his life, and then there would be cake served and people could browse the town's collection of Seigler photos and memorabilia. It all fell together really smoothly. Riley did the introductions, mentally noting that Charley sat a few rows towards the back, just a regular member of town.

Riley introduced Lincoln Ridgton who knew the most about Seigler and would have the longest speech. He sat back down while Lincoln began the same speech they'd all heard for years.

He had to admit he'd been daydreaming after some moments, but the white horse running towards the square seemed real enough. Chief Russell had noted his reaction and then turned to look and then the town saw it as well.

Rennick Halleran was riding bareback through the square on the white horse that had "War" and "Evil" painted in large dark letters on the horse's butt. Rennick was stark naked, shouting and whooping at the crowd as he rode by.

Well, he wasn't completely naked. He had a peace symbol painted on his back.

Chief Russell and his officers took off on foot after Rennick who then lead the horse out of the square. Riley caught a glimpse of Charley who was wiping tears from his eyes he was laughing so hard.

He could only let out a sigh, aware that he had to save the ceremony. He stood up, saying that Seigler would have loved that, and then excused himself to go help catch the horse. Chief Russell could worry about catching his dad.

The horse was running loose when Riley got to the chief. It was spooked, anxiously trying to find a safe route. He got a bucket of feed out of the back of his truck and soon they were able to entice the horse over.

"It has to be from nearby," Riley told Chief Russell. "I doubt my dad hauled it from anywhere."

"I'm going to have to arrest him for that."

Riley nodded. "Do what you have to. I can't control him. Just don't arrest me too," he offered, hoping for a confirmation that he wasn't in trouble as well but Kevin only smiled at him.

"Let me know if you hear from him," the chief said then walked away.

"Great."

Riley's roller coaster day ended quietly enough. He called Greg several times that day, leaving just a message to call him. He wouldn't believe how the day went.

But Greg never called him back.

It bothered him more than it usually would. Normally, he would understand Greg was busy and hadn't perhaps checked his messages, but that night didn't feel that comfortable. He worried that Greg was deliberately not calling him and that made him want to talk to Greg even more, to ensure that they were still okay.

So his next message gave a little bit more detail, wanting to tell what Charley had done and he wouldn't believe what horrible thing his dad had done at the ceremony. That had to be a hook enough to make Greg call.

But he didn't.

So Riley went to sit outside, looking up at the countless stars and listening as a horse ran in the field that he couldn't see. His excitement at being flirted with and his anger at his dad all paled and faded once his uneasy feeling about Greg took hold. He didn't feel anything then but disappointment in himself that he had done something wrong and lost Greg.

Rennick's Irritation

Monday went by empty of contact or excitement. Riley was becoming consumed by his mental game of trying to second-guess Greg's behavior and figuring out what to do next.

It wasn't until Tuesday afternoon that he got a call from Greg.

"I've been busy," was all he offered.

"That's okay," Riley lied.

"What's wrong?"

"Nothing," lying again. "I'm tired."

Greg wanted to know what had happened but all the emotion that had been there was gone and he merely reported the facts of the day and felt disappointed again that Greg didn't pick up on Charley's flirting more. He didn't seem threatened or interested at all.

He summoned up the nerve to finally ask. "Do Charley's actions bother you at all? That he plans to romance me?"

Greg was quiet a bit and then asked, "Do you want to see other people? We could, if that's what you want. I hate to think of you alone, just waiting on me."

"It's not what I want," he replied, angry that Greg didn't even get the point. "And I'm not waiting on you. I'm in love with you."

Greg was quiet again.

He closed his eyes, rubbing his forehead in hopes to end the tension headache that was starting behind his right eye. Was it over? Was he right that he would never see Greg again?

It was a thought that hurt him too much.

"Well," he spoke up, sure he could control his pain, "I'll let you get back to work."

"Okay," Greg whispered, sounding odd himself.

With quick farewells, Riley ended the call. He let out a sigh, burying his face in his hands, wondering if he could wish the whole world away.

The rest of his day was shot. He was so full of bad emotions and doubt that he was becoming almost numb to feeling anything but a huge desire to be physically sick and then needing to crawl into bed, cover up and never leave.

He was aware he was letting himself stare out the window at nothing. There was too much on his mind that needed solutions and he just wasn't able to do it that day. He was tired, disgusted and overwhelmed.

Lost in his mental wandering, it took him an extra second to realize Chief Russell was lightly tapping on his door.

"Sorry," Riley said, quickly standing, hoping to cover the fact he had been daydreaming. Kevin Russell's smile was telling. "Sorry," he said again, feeling he was blushing. "I'm tired."

"You look like it. I won't take much of your time. I just wanted to let you know Strand is out to cause some trouble. He's filed a report with Greene County Sheriff about sabotage in his neighborhood just out of town. Lots of spray paint and things broken, that sort."

"Oh, I think I saw that this weekend."

"You did?"

Riley suddenly felt like he was a suspect. "Yeah. We drove through looking at the houses. I wanted to see how tacky they really were. A couple of them were spray painted."

"Have you seen your father recently?"

"My dad?" Riley asked, feeling again he was confirming his guilt.

"It sounds like something he would do."

"Yeah." He'd thought the same thing. "I haven't seen him, other than the horse escapade."

Kevin nodded, "Okay."

"You're not going to arrest me too, are you?" There was strong panic flowing through Riley's veins suddenly. As if he hadn't had enough trouble to deal with but then add the scandal of being arrested?

"No," Kevin chuckled. "I just told him that I'd arrest you, hoping it would add some guilt to his actions and he might think twice about doing anything."

"He doesn't care about me. He never did."

Kevin nodded, quiet.

"I didn't know his reign of annoyance wandered into other counties either."

"Yep. And if that county catches him, I can't be sure I can help. That Sheriff Struckland is a stickler for the book and we're not really that friendly."

"Great." Riley shook his head, not finding any comfort in the fact that he wouldn't be arrested too. "Well, I haven't seen him and I can't control him so…" he shrugged, giving up.

"Have you seen Charley Claremont?"

"Charley?" Riley asked, instantly filled with an anger at Kevin for participating in the romance game the town seemed to be enjoying.

"They've been spotted around town together some. Thought Miss Charley might know something."

"Oh," he said, aware he'd been thinking wrong. If Russell hadn't dumped enough stress into his life, adding Charley and his dad mixed up in something took Riley underwater and close to drowning. "Great."

Kevin patted Riley's upper arm, smiling, perhaps aware that he had delivered a blow to Riley's stress level. "I'll see you later. Just have your dad contact me if you hear from him again. I want to talk to him before Greene County does."

"Thank you."

One big rule in life, Riley told himself, have friends in high places.

Rennick's location had never been a constant one. His place of residence was usually whichever woman or buddy would let him stay until he had to move on to the next.

Riley's mother had always been the base of the family and when she died, the family seemed scattered and disconnected. Father and son were unable to communicate, other than to argue or ask for money.

Whenever they did meet outside of public places or at a jail, it was a meeting like the one Riley was arranging for them that evening. He drove to the last place he knew his father to have been staying, arriving unannounced with a discussion written and re-written in his head during his travel to the trailer that sat on some land way out of Sleeper's city limits.

His dad opened the door, no real expression on his face, just that he'd been expecting Riley's visit. He stepped out into the warm night wearing only shorts and a cigarette hanging from his lips.

"Figured you'd be showing up."

"You know why then," Riley said, moving to be away from his smoke. His anger at Greg he couldn't express, but his anger at his dad was different. "What the hell was that Sunday?"

"Just an opportunity to express my anger at the war," Rennick replied with no heaviness of guilt.

"It was a chance to land yourself in jail, you know that? They're only going to let you out so many times before they actually make you start serving time. Is that what you want? Prison time? The judge is going to get fed up with seeing you and throw the book at you. It'd just take one parent that was there to press charges and you'd be tried as a sex offender."

Rennick chuckled, like he didn't believe him.

"You'll find out and I won't be able to help you, you know that. Damn it, I'm sick of this. Do you care at all how I felt with everyone knowing that was my dad riding through there buck naked?"

"I waited until your speech was over," he offered like that made it okay.

"Well, thanks then. And I don't suppose I have to ask who painted the peace sign on your back?"

"What?" Rennick snapped, perhaps having not expected Riley to know so much about his doings.

"I know you didn't do that yourself. So who did? Who is going to be going to jail with you?" Riley demanded but in his mind he already knew. Charley had hinted about the fun show to come. He knew.

"I acted alone." Rennick wasn't good at lying.

"And horse stealing? You think that's not a criminal offense?"

"I just borrowed it."

"Right," Riley shook his head. "Chief Russell wants to talk to you *before* the sheriff does."

"Sheriff?" Rennick's expression was full of surprise but then slid away as he knew perfectly well what the sheriff wanted with him. His dad got quiet, like he had lost his nerve for whatever cause he'd been rallying for.

"Maybe you should get some help," Riley finally said, having given up on Rennick's being willing to face Chief Russell.

"Are you sure I'm the one that needs help?"

"Oh, you're saying I do? I'm not out there streaking through town."

"Your life is chaos," Rennick started, a new defensive tone to his voice and actions, like he was pleading his case to the jury. "You've got a hay farm you're allergic to, an old man working with you who might just blow away in the wind, a senile and a blind dog, a horse with OCD, a town that is as kooky as a psych ward with no nurse, a lover that won't speak of your existence."

"Stop!" His dad knew more about his life than Riley had expected. "You forgot a dad that hangs his underwear on flagpoles."

Rennick sighed, then added in a quieter tone, "Don't you see how complicated your life is? You hang on to old things, hoping for miracles. You fight for this old town. You fight against nature for that old farm."

"And live in the old dream of a father?" Riley asked merely to stop his dad's rant. "Tom may be old, but he tries and he doesn't quit. My dogs have been with me forever, why should I abandon them in their old age? The farm is my only source of income, I have to fight for it. My horse cribs but my dad smokes pot, so who's to say which is worse? And I care about this town, kooky or not." He deliberately skipped the line about his lover. "You could help me. You could get back into your life and fight for what you believe through the right channels and have more effect than by streaking through a clown's birthday party. You could have ran for the Senate, you know?"

"Politics is a load of crap. There's no honest men in politics, no way to do the good of the people."

"You think that about me too?"

His dad was quiet for a moment like he'd realized his words had affected Riley wrong. "You won't change anything. One man can't change the system."

"Then work with me and we'd be two."

His dad smirked.

A moment of silence passed between them. Rennick, the man of answers and always open for debate, was silent.

"Know that there's a warrant out for your arrest. I can't help you this time."

Rennick nodded. "Fine. Good night then." He moved back to the trailer's door and stepped inside leaving Riley alone in the yard.

Meeting the Devil

Riley's hometown felt like a foreign town to him. He felt alone in a place that had once been his comfort zone. Most of the town was watching, waiting to hear that the celebrity had wooed the mayor. His dad was escalating his rebellious side and getting more law involved than Riley could help with. His lover had been absent since what Riley had thought had been their best time together. His job was becoming more stressful as the pressure to approve or the growing battle if he didn't approve the rezoning oozed into the mainstream news.

In all these areas, Riley felt he stood alone, with no one to support or help him and that fact made him the saddest of all his other troubles.

But he was in the battle until the end, alone or not. He just wished for a moment's reprieve, perhaps a brief moment that would inspire him to continue the fight. But the moment escaped him.

It was with a downhearted attitude that he headed to lunch that next day. He'd lost sleep after replaying his encounter with his dad and regretting having not said some things to Greg. But it was more than a sleepless night that was fueling his bad mood that day.

Stepping into the café, Riley hoped spending time with his buddies there would help him. It was Charley that he saw first and was aware that he smiled at the celebrity when he entered, but he was suddenly hit with an awareness that his friends were watching them too closely. They went through the motions of greetings and the small talk but Riley could feel the tension around them as they waited to witness some beautiful exchange between himself and Charley.

So Riley did all he could think of. He ordered something quick and to go. He left the café, saying little and didn't look again at Charley. He knew there was a reaction rippling through the crowd he'd left behind.

He walked quickly away from there, catching his breath as he heard the café's door open. He knew Charley was following him but was afraid to look and make it true.

But the quick clop of heels against the pavement confirmed what Riley didn't want to see. Charley was soon at his side, walking with him. "I'm sorry about that," he said.

"About what? You didn't do anything."

"I ran you out of there."

Riley stopped, deciding he didn't want Charley following him all the way back to his office. "They're just waiting for some show and I don't want to be a part of that. I have so much serious stuff to sort through right now, I can't handle their crap."

Charley nodded. "I'm sorry. I never meant to create this."

Riley quickly looked around them, surveying who was watching them but didn't find any onlookers. He let out a deep breath. "I know. I'm sorry. I don't mean to make you feel bad. I'm just in a bad mood and this is too much."

Charley looked at him, his eyes narrowing as if he was scanning Riley's thoughts. "Do I make you uncomfortable?"

He sighed. "I don't know how many times I have to tell you yes," Riley said but there was no anger in his tone.

Charley backed away, rejected. "I do apologize. I didn't mean for this happen."

Riley didn't respond. It wasn't until Charley had taken a few steps that he spoke, "Charley? Try to stay out of my dad's trouble, okay?"

Charley started to say something, perhaps deny any involvement, but he just closed his mouth and nodded. He turned and walked away, returning to the café.

Riley went to his office, no longer hungry for the food before him. Every little thing affected him the wrong way and he hated that but he didn't know how to shut that off.

It had been with the same bad mood that he had taken John Strand's phone call and it was with a deeper darkness that he agreed to meet the man after work. What had led Riley to the meeting with Jonathon Strand he couldn't be sure but he found himself driving the road to the place where Strand's subdivision might be.

Strand was standing beside his Escalade, appearing to be enjoying the country view but Riley guessed he was just plotting out his homes. He parked on the other side of the road and went to Strand's side.

"Mayor Halleran," Strand said, all smiles and warm handshakes, "I was just imagining what your new house will look like."

"Mine?"

"Of course. Who better to have the choice property than the man who helped it be?" Pure salesman tone.

"It's a bit early for that," Riley met the man's eyes.

"I'd hoped to have you on my side. The council will do whatever you tell it."

"I just want the best for my town," he replied, hoping to stop Strand's sales pitch.

"That's what I offer. Affordable housing. Nice luxury homes for the cookie-cutter price. All that business the factory will bring in, you'll be needing homes for the workers." Strand paused a planned beat, then added, " That factory is crucial to your town, isn't it?"

There was something uneasy in his stomach. This was going just as he'd expected. "The factory has nothing to do with land zoning, Mr. Strand."

"No," he shook his head, but his tone was leading to something. "Randall Stanger is a good friend of mine. Takes my advice on all sorts of matters. Even deals that are too good to be true."

"What are you saying?" Riley forced himself to remain in eye contact with the man.

"Simply that Stanger could pull his factory deal if he wanted to. Where would that leave your town? I can take away, or I can give."

"Is that a threat?"

"No. Just the truth. I can raise Sleeper to good heights. Isn't that what you're trying to do? That's all I want."

Riley doubted that. He couldn't prove it but felt the man before him was evil and untrustworthy. "This is something I will have to discuss with council."

"You could decide. They'll follow. We can do the deal right here."

"I'd be impeached," Riley looked out at the land before them. *Gay Mayor Impeached*, he envisioned the headlines. As if one part wasn't enough, his legacy ended with Impeachment. "My answer is no," he looked at Jonathon. "If you can't give me time to think and discuss with the council, then something must be wrong. So the answer is no."

"Nothing is wrong, Mayor Halleran," he laughed like Riley's words were preposterous. "I'm simply a business man who is busy and doesn't have the luxury of time. An opportunity is only as long as its flash, not a moment longer."

"I understand that, but my answer is no."

"Remember I gave you an opportunity. You'll lose sleep over missing out."

Riley smiled, "I have so many problems, Mr. Strand. I'll just add this to the list."

"I'm sure you do," Jonathon looked away. "Rumor has it that your farm might be on the auction block one day."

"What?" Riley was caught off guard by that. "Don't worry about my finances, okay?"

"I could help you keep it," he offered, his tone different than it had been, as if his sweet words were going to sway Riley.

"A bribe? Is that what you're offering?" Suddenly, Riley didn't like being alone out there with that man.

Jonathon was quiet a moment then, "I'm offering my help, is all. I know there's a lot of farms out here in trouble. I can help you all."

"Help us, how? People move to the country to be in the country, not to be three inches from their neighbors. Help the people who want to live in nice country town? It's not by bringing in subdivisions."

"You're making a mistake. Towns do whither and die. You'd be the mayor that coulda saved the town. Be the mayor of a ghost town. Where's the power in that?"

"My life isn't about power. It's about doing the right thing."

"Good. Let's do right thing then," he smiled smugly, like Riley had walked into his trap. "I'll be seeing you at the council's meeting."

Riley sighed knowing Strand thought he was on his side but that wasn't true. He turned to leave, anxious to be away from Strand. He quickly got in his truck, started it and backed up to turn around. He could see Strand still looking out at the field, dreaming of his little empire there.

Getting close to the main highway, he passed a car parked down in the ditch but didn't think anything of it until he got close to the sign Strand had posted about the rezoning. Riley was sure he'd seen someone running to hide. And it came together.

The car in the ditch was Charley's Pacifica and the person he saw running had been Rennick.

Riley slammed on the brakes, letting out an angry breath as he rolled the window down. "I know you're out here!"

Charley slowly stood up from his hiding place. "Hi, Riley," he said, all cheerful, like nothing strange was happening.

"Oh my God," Riley shook his head, moving to park on the side of the road. He got out to meet Charley. "You two are not doing this!"

"Doing what?" Charley winced.

"Strand is just down the road," Riley said. "He is going to catch you! I know my dad is here. Where is he?"

Charley bit at his bright red lips, looking out into the field as he tried to find the correct answer.

"Chief Russell told me he was looking for my dad and that you had been seen with him, so tell the truth. Where is my dad?"

Charley was very uncomfortable, stalling for an answer.

Riley was going to press the issue when he saw Strand's vehicle approaching. He muttered a curse under his breath, feeling every area of his life was about to fall apart.

Strand slowed as he approached the scene. He rolled down his window, smiling as if he knew he was interrupting their little secret meeting. "Good evening, Miss Claremont," he said.

Charley went into pure character, moving to the side of Strand's vehicle, acting like the cameras were on him.

Riley watched the difficult scene, holding his breath that his father wasn't spotted. He wasn't going to look for himself and get caught by Strand who would suspect something was up, despite Charley's convincing story of car trouble and how this was the second time Mayor Halleran had come to his rescue.

Strand offered Riley a direct nod as he slowly moved away, making Riley's already upset stomach ache. He was sure he could feel the ulcers forming.

Charley seemed to be more himself as he moved to Riley's side. "He makes me sick," he said. "What were you two doing out here?"

His question was simple enough but it sent waves of guilt through Riley. "Me? What are you two doing? I know he's here!" Riley shouted to the dark field. He nodded when his dad stepped out from his hiding place. "I knew it. Both of you now. That's just great."

Riley walked away from them, going to his truck.

"I think one would be justified in asking your business out here as well," Rennick said, hurrying up to Riley's side.

"No, I don't think one would be," he replied, mocking his dad's tone. "You two are going to get arrested, do you know that? You'll be responsible for him getting arrested!" he motioned at Charley. "And who will bail you two out?" he dared Charley.

"You didn't tell on us," Rennick said, pointing in the direction Strand had gone.

"I'm not going to but the police know who's doing all this. There's not a real long list of suspects, you know. And now I'm a suspect too because he can place me stopped at the sign that's about to be vandalized."

"Nonsense," Rennick chuckled, but Riley saw him move his hand further behind his back to hide something, presumably a spray paint can.

He looked at the two conspirators, finding himself actually surprised by the situation. His dad's involvement didn't surprise him all that much, but the fact that he'd convinced Charley, a well-know celebrity, to participate did. "You're going to get in so much trouble messing with Strand. Have you thought about the chaos you'll bring into Charley's life if you two get caught?"

"Someone has to stop that land monster before he destroys every tree and patch of Earth."

"There are ways to stop him, dad. Legal ones."

"How? Your way? All meetings and bribes and papers and red tape and bunch of crap? That's all it is, Riley. Crap. You'll never stop these people that are full of the hunger for money. He'd run over you himself if you stood in his way of making money. He offered you a bribe tonight, didn't he? Did you take it?"

"If I did, it was only to cover all the crap you've done."

Rennick shook his head. "He will ruin you, you know that. You go against him, with or without your council, and he will have you impeached before you even know it. He could get the town to run you off. Even your friends will turn against you."

The thought of Strand's retaliation had troubled Riley before. Having the words spoken to him, and in such an angry tone, only solidified his worry. "I will stop him, dad. I will."

"How?" Rennick dared. Riley could only answer with silence. "Exactly," his dad nodded, his point proven.

"Well, you're not stopping him either. All you're doing is getting yourself in trouble until soon you won't be in his way at all anymore because you'll be sitting in the state pen bitchin' about the man that took away your rights. And now you're going to take Charley down with you."

The two fell into silent stares with the always-loud Charley remaining silently in the background, not about to enter that ring.

"I've got to go," Riley sighed. "I've got to work tomorrow." He turned and left the two, not offering anything more. He didn't look in his rearview mirror to see what they were doing. He just wanted to be free of the whole problem.

What made him the most angry after he'd left was the fact that he'd not seen the alliance of his father and Charley. He'd been ready to argue with Chief Russell that there wasn't any way Charley Claremont could be out causing trouble with his dad but he saw what a fool he'd been then.

So why? Why would Charley risk messing up his life to run amuck with a small-time protester and trouble-maker, unless it was the fact that it was *Riley's* dad that was offering the chance.

A Belief About Greg

It was another belief of Riley's about Greg that he called Riley at work when he didn't really want to talk to him. Calls on his cell phone or at home were usually good ones. Most of the calls to the office were either him canceling something or extremely important, although Riley had never received one of those. Calling at work increased the chance of one of them having to cut the call short and the serious topic not having to be discussed.

Riley wanted to be happy when he heard Greg's voice that afternoon but he knew not to expect something good.

Greg's tone was normal at first, asking how things were going in Riley's world. Riley answered simply, not about to go into the details.

"Are we still going to meet next week at Matt's?" he asked, seeming almost innocent of the gash he'd put into Riley's heart days before.

"Okay," Riley agreed. Maybe things were going to be alright after all. "That's fine." Another sexual night with Greg wouldn't be bad, even if he'd never get a husband out of the deal, Riley thought, letting his body make that decision. Next week felt too far away though. Why couldn't they meet that night?

"Okay," Greg agreed. "Um, I'm going to have to get a rain check for our vacation though. Sorry. Something's come up at work."

Riley knew that was a lie and even though it pained him through his being, he told Greg that was fine. They'd reschedule when they could. He knew Greg was blowing him off and he let it happen. He didn't resist, didn't say what he wanted to say.

He closed his eyes, bowing his head, the phone still to his ear, as he half-listened to Greg's concocted story about a work assignment. He wanted to cry but refused to do so as he knew the night at Matt's wouldn't be either.

He hid his pain from Greg, pretending it was fine and fantastic, he'd see him next week, but a tear fell from his eye and rolled slowly down his cheek.

The Specialness of Tom

The weekend was full of plans to help Tom but Riley just couldn't get his mood to anything above polite. He was quiet and Tom let him be so like he understood Riley's need. Tom drove them to town in his flatbed truck, forcing the transmission into third every time. His frail arms still possessed their strength of youth and seemed to be stronger than Riley's that day.

Going through the motions of their tasks in town, Riley tried to help Tom when the old man needed him, tried to keep his aggravation at bay when Tom took too long to make a decision and tried to be polite to the townsfolk that spoke to him. In return, Tom tried to keep Riley free of people wanting his opinion or decision, providing excuses for Riley to step away. They did have a lot of work to get done that day but Riley couldn't get his body and soul to feel connected. He knew he was there but he felt so distant from the situation at the same time.

The day was different. Something was wrong with Riley or with Tom or with the world, he just couldn't decide which or what was wrong. He just simply fell into step beside Tom, let him lead and control while he remained in the shadows. All

Riley could sum up was that he needed a drink and yet he didn't drink.

Tom backed the truck up to the loading ramp at the feed store while Riley helped guide him. He managed to pay attention long enough to not let Tom run the truck into the concrete wall but it was a struggle. He climbed onto the truck's bed with the intention of heading into the warehouse to begin loading the bags of feed for Tom's cows when a car's approach caught his eye.

Charley's Pacifica was navigating the gravel parking lot, careful to miss the pot holes full of rainwater. Riley watched it pass, unable to see Charley inside through the tinted windows. He wasn't sure if it was wishful thinking or his instincts that he thought Charley was watching him as well.

But Riley didn't offer a wave. He just returned to his job of loading the heavy bags. He enjoyed the labor of it. It gave his body something to think about and took the focus off his mind and all the problems swirling there. He had the job of getting all the bags loaded on the truck so none fell off and loaded quickly so the next truck could back in. For a brief moment, it gave him a hint of sunshine in the rainstorm that was consuming him that day.

When the Pacifica pulled in beside their truck, Riley's relief ended. He let the bag on his shoulder fall to the pile, looking at Charley as he stepped out of his car.

Charley's hair was fixed more like he wore it in his shows, spiky and wild. He wore more eye make-up than Riley had seen him wear in town. He wore a yellow tee-shirt that fit tight to his muscular body and jeans. The heels were gone in favor of boots that were still city-boots. The bracelets on his wrists jingled as he reached up to remove his dark sunglasses. His attention was on Riley.

"Hello," he said with a flare to his word.

"Hey," Riley offered, moving the bag he'd dropped into place. Charley came to the edge of the truck by him and looked up at him. "Do you ever think about going into a small town feed store and getting trouble from the guys?"

"No," Charley shook his head. "I don't need to, do I?"

"No, but," Riley stopped himself, unsure what he was trying to say. "Are you just this brave in every situation?"

Charley's concerned look melted into a smile, seeing Riley's question as a compliment. "I'm just buying sand," he said, a deep purr to his voice.

"You realize you stand out?"

Charley's smile then was ornery. "You were worried about me?"

"No. Just curious if you're always so bold."

"You should know the answer to that," Charley said. He moved to the stairs and walked onto the platform where Riley and Tom loaded the bags. "Do we have to load our own or is there someone?"

"There's a guy back there," Tom answered. "But we can load it for you."

Riley looked at him, letting out a disgusted breath.

"Ignore him," Tom waved his hand in Riley's direction. "He's just in a mood."

"I see that. Troubles in Riley World?" Charley asked, his words no doubt supposed to lighten Riley's mood but it only forced him a bit more back into his rainstorm.

He shook his head, moving away, grabbing another bag of feed, excusing himself from that scene, letting Tom entertain his new friend. He'd just load the bags, they could analyze his life for him.

Who could say, Riley thought later after he worked out some of his anger, maybe they'd find the answer that was alluding him.

They loaded the truck and then Charley's sand. Riley returned back to his robotic day, offering Charley a farewell but his heart and mind were somewhere else.

He got in the truck, fastening his seatbelt as Tom started the engine. Tom watched Charley drive off before he put the truck in gear and followed Charley out of the parking lot and then onto the outer road to the highway.

"You should be nicer to him, you know?"

"What?" Riley asked, not able to comprehend that his friend was beginning a lecture.

"He likes you."

"So?" Riley asked, any further argument leaving him. He could only shrug and then look out the window. "I don't need any more crap," he sighed.

"True," Tom said. "You need something *good*," he said, his words spoken deliberately. He wasn't arguing, wasn't lecturing. He was simply trying to tell Riley something he wouldn't let himself understand.

Riley remained quiet for most of the ride. He wasn't angry at Tom or at anyone and he hoped he wasn't giving off that vibe. He was just so tired. He'd turned things over in his mind so many times and still didn't have any answers, only more questions and troubles.

They stopped to get gas before heading home. Riley remained in the truck while Tom pumped the gas and chatted with the man at the other pump about how cattle prices were going to run them out of the business. Tom went inside to pay after a short discussion and returned with a cold soda he handed to Riley.

"Thanks," he said sheepishly, feeling sorry for snapping at Tom earlier.

Tom just smiled at him, nodded, and started the old truck and headed them for home. The cold drink was helping to bring some clarity to Riley's gray day and he was beginning to feel more comfortable in Tom's presence.

So when they came to a top of a hill and could see Charley's Pacifica pulled over towards the side of the gravel road, Riley could only let out a quiet sigh. He looked at Tom then, wondering if they'd arranged this meeting.

But the purely frustrated look on Charley's face told Riley it hadn't been planned.

Tom parked behind the car and they moved to meet Charley at the side. Charley's frustration was covered up by his embarrassment as he looked at Riley. "At least it's a different tire," he said, his tone trying to make it a good thing.

"Do you have a spare?" Riley asked, deciding to just get Charley on the road again himself instead of messing with finding someone to come help.

"Yeah," he nodded, pushing a button on the remote to open the back hatch. "Good thing I got the other tire fixed."

Riley agreed but he regretted his offer when he saw the bags of sand they had loaded not long ago. He wanted to cuss but he just sighed.

Nothing said between them, the three of them began unloading the sand. Getting the tire iron and jack free, Tom took them from Riley's hands. "I'll do it."

"No," Riley said, not comfortable with asking Tom to do such a heavy job with two younger guys standing and watching.

"Nonsense," Tom said, going to the tire like there was to be no discussion about it.

Tom doing the work left Riley and Charley to stand facing each other. Riley nervously drank his soda.

Guessing there was only going to be silence between the two must have encouraged Tom to start talking. His questions were directed at Charley, knowing all of Riley's secrets and perhaps leaving Riley to remain in the state he'd been in all day.

"Are you liking our small town, Charley?"

"Yes," Charley answered quickly, as if he'd not been expecting the attention. "I am actually. Met quite a few wonderful people. It's nice."

"Probably different than that big Hollywood town, huh?" Tom smiled at Charley.

"A lot, yes. Part of what I like about it."

"Going to be staying long?"

"Um," Charley looked anxiously at Riley. Either his answer was one he didn't want Riley to know or it depended on Riley's response. "I'm here for awhile," he replied, looking down at Tom. "Then I'll just stay when I'm not working. Lots of traveling," he said, looking quick to catch Riley's eyes then away.

Riley offered a small smile, feeling he needed to respond in some form, but his smile was forced. It hadn't occurred to him that Charley would be leaving them. That fact affected him more than he thought it would.

"Well, I'm no world-class chef but I'd like to invite you to dinner. My wife and I always have an anniversary dinner and I want all our best friends to be there. That would include Riley here and you, if you'd be interested."

"Certainly," Charley answered but Riley heard the uncertainty in his voice. "Just let me know when."

Tom nodded.

"I'd bet your wife is a lovely woman," Charley said.

"She was," Tom said, a distant tone to his words.

"Was?" Charley asked, tilting his head as he looked at Riley.

Riley could only offer a smile to a perplexed Charley.

"She passed away some time ago, but we still have dinner on our anniversary. My wedding day was the absolute best day in my life."

Charley's smile then was one of respect and perhaps a bit of longing to feel the same way. "That is so touching and romantic. I'd be honored to be a part of that."

"Alright. I'll set a place at the table."

An awkward silence settled then and Riley felt obligated to get them talking again. It was his way to apologize to the two for being so distant that day. "What do you have planned for all this sand?"

"I'm planning on redoing the back yard at my house. I'd love to have a pond and waterfall and a nice patio to enjoy the stars on. But I'm just landscaping right now, doing some small things."

"You like that sorta stuff?"

"Oh, yes. I love getting my hands in the soil and growing stuff."

"I didn't know that."

"These hands," Charley said, holding his hands up and turning them to look at both sides, "are good for more than chopping carrots," he said.

Riley studied Charley's hands quickly, finding himself wondering what else those hands had done; how many men they had touched.

"Grow a garden?" Tom asked, his attention on the tire.

"Normally I do. I won't plant one here until next Spring. Too much to do before I start taking care of a garden. I hope you like tomatoes," he said, looking at Riley. "I can definitely grow tomatoes. I just can't eat them fast enough."

"Rie?" Tom called from the tire, "Can you take these?"

Riley moved to take the lug nuts from Tom. He wanted to change the tire himself, not because of the guilt he'd felt earlier, but to speed things along. He was running out of small talk and he dreaded the subject of Greg coming up.

"Rie," Charley said once that was done. "I like that."

Riley shrugged. "Just a nickname."

They stood in silence for a moment, their eyes locked in a comfortable stare. Riley broke the contact, looking down, smiling and feeling embarrassed.

There was silence between them then with the feeling that questions about Greg were being avoided, despite Charley's wanting to ask.

Riley thought about asking if Charley had caused any more trouble with his dad but he chose to avoid that subject as well.

"So how long were you married?" Charley asked, moving back to Tom's side and focusing on him.

"It will be sixty-one years this year."

"Wow. That's fabulous."

Although Riley felt himself connected once again to his surroundings, he let himself remain out of the conversation that began between Tom and Charley. Tom told the story of his and Olive's life together, sharing the highpoints and then ending with

Olive's death. Riley just watched the two's interaction, seeing Charley's interest was real, his eyes filling with tears as Tom spoke of Olive's leaving him.

It was a special moment that Riley witnessed and it made him smile to know that Tom found someone worthy of sharing his story with and that Charley was honestly touched by it. He didn't feel bad about being left out of the conversation, but wondered if the distance he'd felt all day was just preparing him for the moment before him. It was a chance to witness something magical.

When the tire was changed and the flat tire and bags of sand loaded, the three parted ways comfortably enough. Riley was quiet on the rest of the ride to Tom's house but he wore a smile on his face, still touched by the simple moment that had affected him and also allowing Tom to remain in whatever memory of Olive held him.

A Healing Afternoon

The trip to town early that next morning had been an inconvenience but he had been craving chocolate ice cream since Tom had left him the day before. Headed home to a long day of boring laundry and anxiousness about each phone call (Would it be Greg or some other issue to deal with?), Riley had to laugh as he came upon the familiar sight of the Pacifica pulled over to the side.

He slowed down, coming to a stop at the driver's window, smiling at Charley who stood outside, his head bowed. "You have money, yes?" Riley asked.

"Yes," Charley answered as if unsure where Riley's questioning would lead.

"Will you go today and buy yourself some decent tires? I can't keep cruising the roads rescuing you."

Charley's smile was sweet. "I owe you."

Riley nodded, moving to turn the truck around and then park behind Charley's car.

"I'm beginning to think you do this on purpose," he said with no threat to his tone as he walked to meet Charley at the back of the car.

Charley could only smile as if there was no excuse he could offer. "Will you help me?" His expression became more pained. "You're really going to hate me." He opened the back hatch to show the treasure there: bags and bags of potting soil and decorative rocks. "I was going to do some landscaping."

"You are out to kill me, aren't you."

"Sorry."

"We can load this in my truck. Probably wouldn't be good for your fake tire. Or we can call a tow truck." Riley knew the answer but he gave the offer anyway.

"I'll fix you lunch," Charley offered.

The farmhouse that Charley had bought was a beautifully remodeled place that had been a spectacular mansion in the town in its day, long before huge houses were built all the time. He hadn't changed the place much, other than to add a lot of plants on the porch and make the house feel cozy and welcoming.

Charley opened the front door and let Riley pass. The rooms were still full of boxes, some unpacked, some empty and laying flat in the corner. "Sorry," Charley said. "I'm just getting around to moving in. The kitchen is fully functioning though."

"It's okay. You don't have to fix lunch."

"I want to. I owe you for saving me once again. I owe you a lot, actually," Charley said, his tone dropping like those words were full of more honesty than the others. "Here," he said, reaching to take the ice cream from Riley. "I'll put this up."

"Thanks."

Charley hit the button on his answering machine that announced he had twenty-seven messages as he returned from the kitchen and putting the ice cream in the freezer. The first message started but didn't seem to hold Charley's interest. "It'd be great to have them by that tree in the front yard. Let me check these and change and I'll help you."

Second message was Eddie, his agent. The third, fourth and fifth messages were him as well. Several more from friends and ones that meant something to Charley but no details were offered to Riley. Then more from Eddie, whose tone was growing more urgent with each message. Charley winced, "I'd better call him."

A phone in another room began to ring. Charley just waved his hand, concentrating on the messages.

"Let me call him first," Charley said when the messages were done.

"That's fine. I can unload. You do what you have to."

A phone rang somewhere in the house.

"How many phones do you have?"

"Um...seven I think. I only give important people my private number though," he said, holding up his cell phone. "Helps me weed out all this other crap. I'll hurry. Fix yourself something to drink, have a snack, whatever. Make yourself at home."

Charley disappeared into the back room while Riley was left to wander into the kitchen. That room was definitely the spirit of Charley. It was spacious and full of natural light. There was no clutter to be seen, no cookware or dirty dishes. Everything had its place and it all seemed to center around a photograph hanging on the wall of Charley and an older woman cooking that Riley guessed to be Charley's mother.

He could hear Charley's voice every so often, possibly arguing with Eddie. He was saying something about not caring if it was the cover, he wasn't doing it.

Riley was searching through the obviously expensive refrigerator when Charley joined him.

"I am so sorry," he smiled. "I have an interview scheduled that I have to do."

"That's fine, really. Do what you need to do."

"Will you stay? I *will* fix you lunch."

Stay? There was his opportunity to simply unload the bags and leave and not have to be alone with Charley, but Riley found himself saying that he would stay. "It's fine. Do your interview. I'll unload the truck."

"You're a dear," he said, reaching out and quickly patting Riley's arm. He then returned to the back room which Riley guessed was Charley's office.

He unloaded the truck then returned to the kitchen. He washed his hands then fixed himself a soda, listening to Charley's interview, aware that the celebrity Charley Claremont was in the other room. He was in pure character, a bit of arrogance to his voice that was a side effect of having the spotlight on him.

Riley listened and waited.

He tried not to snoop in Charley's things but he was growing bored. Part of the living room had been set up. There were photographs in frames on the coffee table and the fireplace mantel. He looked at them, getting glimpses of Charley's private life that he knew nothing about. One man appeared in two of the photos with Charley who was clearly more than a friend. There were several of Charley onstage and studio shots and then one very artistic one of the man Charley really was. It was a black and white of him shirtless, without makeup, looking down like he was sad. That photo kept Riley's attention for a few minutes too long.

He decided that he would find something to eat and start cooking, even though he was in a chef's territory.

Riley looked up to see Charley standing in the doorway, his hand over his heart, his mouth hanging open. "You're cooking?"

"Yeah," he answered, not sure if he'd broken some big rule and offended Charley or if it was a good thing. He was very relieved to see the smile that spread across Charley's face.

"I don't think a man has ever cooked for me," he said stepping up to Riley's side. "It smells great."

"It's nothing fancy, nothing of your caliber."

"Posh," he waved his hand again like Riley's worries were nothing. "It's fabulous." Charley smiled sweetly at him. Riley got the impression that he was so moved by his cooking that Charley was going to cry. Had no one really ever cooked for him?

"Your cell phone's been going off a lot."

"Oh, I'm sure. They all go non stop. With you here, I'll turn them all off so we don't have to hear them."

"Is it always like this?"

"Oh yeah. Imagine what it's like at my house in California, where people know where I am. They can just show up at the door. You see why I ran away to a small town no one could find if they wanted to."

"I see. I don't know how you take it."

"I don't, sometimes." Charley turned his phone off.

"Well, I'm glad to know I'm not the reason for you being here."

Charley looked at him, a small smile on his face. "You were the deciding factor on my destination, but not the reason for me coming, no. You don't have to worry about that."

Charley moved to the fridge and fixed himself a drink.

"If my ice cream is still any good, we can have it for dessert," Riley offered, tending to the mix of chicken and sauce in the skillet.

"Great. I think it survived. I promise I will go tomorrow and get tires. They will be made out of metal if I can find that."

Riley smiled, a want in him to tell Charley he didn't mind being needed after all, for changing tires or fixing dinner. After tending to the chicken, he looked at Charley, finding a slyness about Charley that had just appeared.

"Would you like a tour?"

There was a hint of nervousness inside Riley as he followed Charley into the living room, aware that the tour was going to move past bedrooms and he wasn't certain what he would do if Charley made a pass at him. He wasn't totally against the idea of giving in to the celebrity if that did happen.

Charley pointed to one of his show posters, announcing that was his favorite one of all his work photos. It was an image of him in his signature heels, leather pants and tight shirt standing amongst a city with an attitude like he owned the place and a sparkle in his eye that showed his mischievous side. Concert dates were listed down the side but Riley's eyes couldn't fall on anything but Charley's daring eyes.

"I'm curious about this one," he said as they approached the one that held his attention earlier.

"That? Well, that was just a friend of mine who did photography playing around one day. We did several of these, real serious ones," Charley said, posing again, "and some funny ones. Ones with Drag. Ones like these, just me."

"I like this. You look very handsome without the makeup. You look great with it too, but I just never thought about how you looked without it. Lots of muscles too."

"Stop," he smiled, "you're making me blush."

Riley laughed.

"I'll get one for you. Have it blown up. Maybe I'll stop wearing the make-up, romance you that way."

"Charley," Riley sighed. "It's not about romancing me and I definitely don't want to be the one responsible for ruining your career by making you take off the makeup. I like it. I'm just saying you look really good without it too."

"Thank you," he said sincerely.

"You're welcome." They moved to the next photo. "Who's this guy?"

"That is my ex-husband."

"Husband?"

"Oh yeah. I'm a homebody. I want to be the housewife. I'm not one to be out playing around and all wild. I'm not the celebrity in that aspect. We were together for a while before I really got famous. We had a ceremony three months after we got together and I thought we would be together forever."

"What happened?"

"I got famous," Charley said sadly. "He said it was my working, that I'd changed, that he didn't feel good enough. Oh, it was all kinds of things really. Essentially, it was an ego conflict, he sapping all my money for his little flings, and the cheating."

"Sorry."

"Well, I can't blame him, I guess. He was alone a lot. He never really was supportive of my career from the beginning, until I got famous and then he was Mr. Charley, you know, parading around. Which is understandable. I was having fun being famous too. We just didn't work out."

"Do you still talk to him?"

"No." Charley seemed sad about that but the sadness seemed to have faded into memory.

"Sorry. I didn't mean to bring you down. I was just wondering if he was your boyfriend or not."

"If I was single?" Charley smiled, clearly turning the conversation away from the ex.

"Yes," Riley admitted.

"I am. I don't have a lot of boyfriends to brag about. I don't pick up men after my shows. I'm not promiscuous. I don't have the time or the energy," he smiled.

"No. Only time to answer phones," Riley teased.

Charley nodded. "See why I like to spend a lot of my time outdoors?"

"I thought my phone was aggravating but seven?"

Charley shrugged. "I've gotten used to it. Want to see my mess outside I've been doing in-between flat tires?"

Riley followed Charley back past the kitchen, getting a quick glimpse of Charley's office and out the back door to the deck. The back yard was decorated with flowers and several small ponds. A walkway was beginning to take shape into the back corners of the yard, through the arrangements of flowers and tranquility Charley was clearly out to design.

"Wow," Riley smiled. "I never would have thought of you doing this."

"I wouldn't have thought of you being such a good cook," he replied, "which we'd better go check on."

They hurried back to the kitchen, finding dinner ready.

It was awhile after they started eating and the small talk began to pass that the subject of Greg was mentioned.

"You probably don't want to discuss it but it's looming over me and I just want to get it over with. How are you and Greg?"

Riley's first reaction was to get defensive and refuse to discuss it but there was a much bigger part of him that wanted someone to talk to. "I'm not sure. We have a date next week but things haven't been all that great recently. We had a vacation scheduled the end of this month and he cancelled out on me. I think I know how we are but I don't want to face it."

"I'm sorry. I can see that hurts you."

Riley took a drink of wine, smiling. He let the thought of Greg come and go. Greg wouldn't care that he was sitting at dinner with another man. "What about my dad? He doing okay?"

"As spirited as ever."

"Don't help him, please? I don't want you to get in trouble for his mess."

Charley looked away like he wasn't worried about that possibility.

They fell into a silent moment, avoiding looking at each other.

"I can't believe I'm sitting at the dinner table of Charley Claremont," Riley confessed. "When I think of who you really are it freaks me out."

"I'm just Charley. I can't believe I'm sitting here with you."

"Why am I so special?"

Charley smiled, a hint of blush to his face. "You just are."

"You know so much about me. How'd you ever hear of me? I'm just a small town mayor."

"You're openly gay though. I read about you in a magazine when you were first elected."

Riley nodded, aware there had been a brief flash across the gay world of his election but it hadn't amounted to anything.

"I was curious what this openly gay mayor looked like so I looked for articles. Finally found a link to the paper here and I've read it religiously ever since I saw a photo of you. I can't say why, just that you got my attention and I've stayed interested all this time

"I was about to have a nervous breakdown in my life earlier this year. I've been stretched so thin and so many people trying to get my attention and affection and I just couldn't handle it anymore. I thought, 'How nice it would be to just live a simple life in a simple town.' And it just hit me square on the head. 'Take a bloody vacation'," he smiled. "There was just one place in the world I wanted to go and here I am. You led me to this place but I really didn't come with the aspiration of romancing you. I apologize for coming on so strongly. I want to thank you for allowing me to escape the hell of the world I live in and I do apologize if I've darkened yours."

"You haven't darkened mine. I couldn't figure out why you ended up here. Maybe the pressure of the idea of you being here for me was too much."

"Well relax, I'm not. Meeting you just was a pleasant side effect of escaping. May I just say you are more wonderful than I had imagined."

Riley smiled at him, not prepared to respond to that. He took another sip of wine, letting the words linger between them. "So you are going to go back to that hell?"

"Sort of," Charley winced. "I'll go tape my shows, do what I have to do but I'm not going to tour or do the interview circuit like I'd planned. I'm going to slow things down a bit. My agent isn't about to let my fire burn out though." Charley loaded his fork and took a bite but Riley felt there was something more he'd wanted to say.

"Well," Riley said after a few bits of quiet, feeling the need to say something, "we're all glad you're here."

Charley's smile then seemed to ease a lot of his unspoken troubles. "I am cooking for the ladies and whoever wants to come the last Saturday of this month. I'd love for you to come. They want me to do a show for them, teach them how to cook something, so I gave in," he rolled his eyes like they had really had to talk him into it.

Riley didn't have an excuse ready. "Um, I'll just have to see."

"I'd like for you to be there. It'll just be dinner, drinks, a few of my jokes. Nothing major. No camera crews," he added quickly like he'd feared Riley had suspected a set-up to be on his show.

"Thanks. I'll try," he said when he wanted to confirm he'd be there and yet didn't want to go at the same time.

"Great," Charley smiled, the date confirmed to him.

The rest of dinner and dessert had passed with small talk or polite questions. Riley helped him clear the table but Charley refused to let him clean up.

It was in the awkward moments after that Riley felt the need to leave Charley's world. The parting was friendly but Riley felt they both hadn't honestly wanted it to happen, as if Charley didn't want to return to his world or let Riley get away from him.

Riley drove home feeling good about his afternoon, even if he didn't get all his laundry done, and didn't worry that he'd sent the wrong message to Charley by spending the day with him. There had just been a nice afternoon spent together, whether it was the forming of a friendship or something more it didn't matter. It had been a healing afternoon.

Annette's Advice

Sitting bored at work that next day, Riley decided to do something he hadn't done since Charley arrived there. He put Charley's name in the search engine online and took in Charley's official website and then several of the fan-based sites. He looked at photos of Charley's past and put pieces together of the mystery Charley had been to him. Charley the celebrity Riley knew. He vacationed at ski resorts, was a friend to a princess that had died in a plane crash, and had been in several movies as characters totally not like the person he knew Charley to be.

But the human Charley had family and friends and an ex-husband. He'd gone to chef school and struggled to make ends meet. He'd broken a leg snowboarding. He'd been in a car crash in New York. He'd worked hard to make it as a comedian and to be accepted even though he liked to wear women's clothes. He wasn't a drag queen out doing bar shows. He was just a gay man that preferred heels to comfortable shoes. He spoke fluent French and did beautiful works of art. He owned a farm in Riley's town.

"Are you busy?"

Riley looked up to see Annette standing at his door. "Not really. Come in." He closed the site as Annette approached but he knew he'd been caught already.

She sat across from him, sitting a candy bar on his desk. "I thought it might be break time."

"Thanks."

She smiled at him in a way that he knew she'd seen what he was looking at. "Checking out Charley?"

"Yes," he confessed, not wanting to fight it. "Curious about him. I've been invited to a cooking date at the end of the month. You are going, aren't you?" he asked, knowing she was one of the women invited.

"I'd planned on it but if you're going to be there then definitely. See the sparks ignite," she teased.

"Don't start," he shook his head but his defensiveness about Charley wasn't there.

"Do you like him?" she asked as if she was surprised by his change in attitude.

"He's nice. He's funny."

"I mean *like* like."

He thought about saying his usual response but he found himself being quiet. He looked out the window, trying to make his heart think about Greg but those thoughts only made him angry.

"I can't deny that having a celebrity interested in me isn't flattering. Just having a handsome man interested in me is flattering. Someone that pays attention to me."

"Handsome," she smiled, like his word had pleased her. She then grew serious, "You and Greg having problems?"

"Isn't that all we've ever had?" he smiled. "I'm the other woman, of sorts. I get to see him when he says."

"I think you deserve more than that." Her dislike of Greg had never been a secret.

Riley shrugged. "I just want to wake up with someone, eat meals with someone, know he'll be home when I get home. I want a relationship I guess. I don't want to be the mistress."

"Ditch Greg then and be with Charley."

Riley looked down. The words made it seem so simple but it wasn't. "I want that with Greg," he softly confessed. He looked at her then away again. "But I don't think I'll ever see Greg again."

Annette sighed, "Sorry. If it helps, I would love to have a wild, spontaneous sex life over a marriage. You want companionship. I'd like to have sex."

Riley smiled, letting the focus move away from him. "No sex in marriage?"

"Not after eighteen years there isn't. At least not with me," she added, distant.

They smiled at each other, letting their own desires and pains fade.

"Anyway," Riley continued, "Charley's a celebrity. Has a big life out there. Not like I have anything to offer him here."

"Sure you do. Beautiful blue eyes, nice bod and hair, stable life."

"How does that compare?"

"Compare to fake, money-hungry users?"

He nodded, feeling her words were true. Charley had voiced his disgust at his life just the day before. "Who's to say I'm not just starstruck and he's the type to take advantage of that? I'm so messed up about Greg I may be misreading my own feelings."

"Well, I guess just enjoy it while it lasts, then. Get to say you had sex with a celebrity."

Riley laughed, feeling his face blush. "I can't get past him being a celebrity though. It's so bizarre. The man on TV is the same guy out there with flat tires."

She looked at him oddly but didn't question him further. "You know your eyes light up when you talk about him?"

"That could just be the starstruck thing."

"So you're going to hold out for Greg to come to his senses and sweep you off your feet?"

Riley smiled, knowing that was exactly what he was waiting for. "I fell in love with Greg the instant I saw him."

"I know, sweet, or you wouldn't let him treat you so badly. He's not proving to be worthy of you," she said with a delicate tone. "He's not going to be with you 'til death do you part."

"And Charley would be?"

"I don't know. I just think he'd treat you better even in a short amount of time than Greg has in how many years?"

Riley looked at his desk, knowing her words could be true.

"Let Greg go. I know it hurts but let your heart and mind let go of him. I'm not saying run to Charley, I'm just saying release yourself so when the real love comes along you won't be inhibited, waiting for this miracle from Greg that isn't going to be."

Riley felt his sadness return to him and fought to keep the tears from his eyes. "I think Greg is arranging that for me. He's cancelled our vacation and I bet you he cancels our date for this week. It just hurts more than I want it to." He looked out the window in hopes he could keep his emotions in check. "I have so much anger at him for this, for not being who I wanted, for stringing me along all this time, for not even trying to love me. I think that's what's affecting me more than anything."

"So call him, unload all this on him."

"I can't. I just clam up and say nothing. Me, political debater able to argue a point for anything and I can't tell him the simplest thing." He shook his head, breathing through his anger as he forced it away. "It's fine," he continued, "we'll just part in silence and I'll one day forget why I loved him so much."

Annette nodded, smiling. "You will because you'll find someone that makes you happy and you won't give a crap about the jerk you used to date."

"I hope so but," he shrugged, "right now I'm just gonna hide in here and surf the net and wait for the horrible council meeting come up."

"Don't worry about it," she said, standing. "I've got your back and I always have two shoulders to cry on and a freezer full of ice cream."

Riley smiled, grateful she was his friend. "I may be in need of both shoulders and all the ice cream real soon. We might add some Jack Daniels to that list."

Annette offered him a sympathetic smile. "It'll work out. You'll see."

Charley's Magic

It hadn't occurred to Riley that his town was changing until the evening when he went to the store to get a few things before heading home after work. It was the sight of Beatrice Anderson and Olivia Howell walking down the store aisle together filling up the cart Olivia pushed that stopped Riley in his tracks and he understood then the strange calm that had arrived in his town.

Beatrice and Olivia had been at war as long as Riley could remember. It would be boundary lines or city ordinances or some stupid idea that would get a call to the police or county commissioner. There was a year of their legally fighting to disallow dog owners to live in their neighborhood. The two neighbor ladies couldn't like the others dogs, one with two Great Danes, one with five Pomeranians. They'd fought over driveway colors, political candidates, handicap parking spaces put in at the fast food place near the highway. They had never, in well over Riley's thirty years, spoken a friendly word to the other.

And they were getting groceries that day like best friends. Both were smiling and pleasant to the shoppers around them.

Riley knew who had been the peace mediator between the long-time enemies and as he thought the name Charley, the actual man walked past the end of the aisle. There was a small basket dangling from his arm that held his few selections. His head was held high as he took large steps past the aisles. His outfit was still the city-celebrity he was but all that stood out was his high heels.

And then tailing behind him were three ladies, walking quickly like they didn't want Charley to escape. They too carried baskets that seemed to contain the same items Riley had noted in Charley's.

He watched them walk on by, then tried to listen where they had gone. Curious about this new store game and still amazed at the impossible duo shopping before him, Riley didn't hear Charley come up behind him and jumped when he greeted him.

"Sorry," Charley smiled.

"I was just…" he let his sentence drop, deciding he didn't want to admit he had been wondering where Charley had gone. He waved his hand, shrugging.

"I can feel the tension around you," Charley said, falling into step beside Riley as they moved on down the aisle.

"It's been a stressful day," he said, not looking at the man beside him that epitomized carefree happiness.

The group of women turned the corner of the aisle as if in a panic that they had lost Charley. Finding themselves caught, they quickly stopped to look at the boxes of rice at the end.

"Do you know…" Riley started, not too sure how to finish that either. He could only nod back at the ladies.

"Oh yeah," Charley smiled, wrinkling his nose and shaking his head. "I get a kick out of it." He reached over and grabbed a can of something and threw it in his basket. As they moved on out of the aisle, Riley noted the women stopped and got the same item. Charley quietly laughed.

They walked a few steps more, listening to the women's talk on the aisle over. Riley tried to think of something to say but all his ideas seemed silly. He merely just walked with Charley, feeling like he was on show since the whole town knew about Charley's intentions and that added troubles to his already full mind. Would people think they were already together?

When he decided on something harmless to say, he and Charley both began talking at the same time. With smiles, they each told the other to go first. It wasn't until the appearance of Bernard Hugo that they fell silent.

Bernard walked past the aisle, not seeming to notice them. He was an older man, always very quiet, very stern looking. He had been a war vet, decorated hero he would tell it. Shot down, barely survived. What made him unique to the town was the burned side of his face, his "war wounds."

The sight of Bernard stopped Charley, making Riley stop to look at him. Charley's expression was full of thought, his lips puckered, his eyebrows furrowed. "Was that…Was he…"

Riley nodded, "Wearing a mask? Yeah." The burns were as fake as the stories.

"It's a mask?"

He nodded again. Another one of his cases loose in the psych ward.

The two continued on, Charley obviously still quietly trying to get his mind around Bernard's psychosis and Riley beginning to get comfortable with the man beside him. A sweet Muzak song played over the intercom above them. It was a scene out of movie, he thought, a sweet little interlude at the store.

The mood of the store was infecting. Everyone there seemed to be at peace, happy and moving through the same musical interlude Riley felt himself to be in. And the star of it, the man at his side, moved through it all seeming to take no note of his effect.

Several aisles down, Charley's little basket ended up in the cart Riley pushed. Their selections were made with comfortable small talk, all the while Riley took note of the difference he saw in people around him.

At one point, Charley stopped in mid-aisle and looked at Riley with a gleam in his eyes that made him fear he was about to be pounced on. "I know just what you need," he said, his eyes wide and a huge smile on his face. "Cookies!"

At the register, Charley insisted on paying for everything and Diane the clerk didn't think twice about it. At Charley's car, they separated their bags and he promised to deliver Riley his life-altering cookies that Saturday morning since Riley said he was too busy for company before then. They then loaded Riley's bags and then Charley headed back to his car.

Riley watched the graceful man walk away, saw him wave at a few people who offered greetings like friends. Charley Claremont had changed the town but the town had changed Charley too. He noticed the storm about Charley was beginning to calm. Charley the Celebrity was becoming Just Charley, flamboyant, boisterous and funny still, but it was no longer demanded attention about him.

While he'd found Charley abrasive at first, this new Charley didn't seem so bad. This Charley was caring and humorous and handsome and the town was beginning to take him in like family.

Riley

He watched Charley drive away, the whole time wanting to ask Charley to stay for as soon as he had started walking away, the burdens of Riley's life returned and he felt alone and unhappy once again.

It was only driving past Tom's house that Riley was able to stop thinking about his life and his night. It occurred to him then that he was supposed to have had dinner with his friend.

Riley called as soon as he got inside his home. "I'm sorry. I stopped at the store and ran into Charley and it took longer than I thought and I just forgot."

He heard the smile in Tom's voice as he said, "Ah, Miss Charley."

"Don't start," Riley sighed but he was smiling too. "You just have a good dinner. I'll see you later, okay?"

"Okay. I heard they arrested your dad."

"They did? I hadn't heard. Guess I'll be getting a call then. But, you just go enjoy your dinner. I'll see you later."

He went about his night, still consumed by all the stresses he'd allowed in, but the phone call he kept waiting for never came.

Much More

So swept up in his business dealings that morning, it took Riley a moment to realize that it was Greg on the phone. It caught him off guard and when Greg said he couldn't make their date the next night it surprised him even though he'd expected Greg to cancel.

"Fine," Riley said shortly. "I've got to get to a meeting," he lied.

"Okay. I'll call you later?"

"Fine," he said. "Later." He hung up, catching his breath and holding it for a moment. He slowly released it, aware that what he'd dreaded happening was really taking place. Greg had cancelled as expected and Riley's heart broke freshly, having been holding onto his dream that Greg would come through.

His emotions physically under control, he decided to walk off his anger. He went up the stairs and then back down to the basement, not caring if anyone did witness what could have been considered indecision.

He went to the vending machine and bought a candy bar, hoping the chocolate would ease his emotions but doubting it would. He returned to his office with the last bit of emotion being stomped out in the stairway. Entering his office, he was unprepared to find a man standing at the window. "Geez," he sighed, shaking his head as Charley turned to smile at him.

"Wondered where everyone was. Meeting?"

"No," Riley reported, moving to his desk, opposite of the side Charley stood at. "Just went to get a snack."

"Those are horrible for you," Charley winced at the candy bar.

"I know but it tastes good." He tossed the candy bar to his desk with an edge of anger, not sure if he wanted Charley to know his real reason for getting the candy or if he just wanted to pretend he was fine.

He wanted to ask why Charley was there but all his questions would lead to an inappropriate answer or were just plain rude. *Something I can do for you? Why do I get a visit? Why are you here?*

"Did you know," Charley asked, pointing at the window, "that some guy just drove the wrong way around the square? Nearly hit two cars."

"Oh yeah. That's Mr. Crenshaw. He does that all the time so beware if you're heading around the square in the morning or after lunch."

"Why does he do that?"

"Well, his store is right there at the end and he refuses to drive all the way around the square when his store is right there. So he just turns left in and up a bit and he's at his store. Others, beware."

Charley's face formed in the same thoughtful frown Riley had witnessed over Bernard Hugo's mask, like a rational man couldn't understand the quirks of Riley's oddball town. "Well, anyway," he sighed, turning his full attention to Riley. "I brought you something."

"Charley—"

"—Nonsense," he waved Riley's words away. He went to the chair near the door and lifted up a large rectangular present. He handed it over. "Open it."

Riley carefully tore at the white wrapping paper, finding brilliant colors of orange, yellow, white and red painted on the canvas beneath it. The colors blended into each other like a burst of energy.

"Thank you," he said, looking at Charley whose smile beamed.

"There's a whole story behind it but I'll tell it to you another day, not right now." He had a slight blush to his cheeks.

"This is fantastic. You're quite a Renaissance Man, huh?'

Charley shrugged, smiling. "Then you're my muse. I had a great time painting it. I hope you enjoy it."

"I do. It's beautiful." No one had ever given him art before and now Charley had done two things for him. "Thank you."

"You're welcome," Charley replied with a hint of humor at Riley's repeated thanks.

"When do I get to hear the story? I'm curious now."

"Oh, maybe one day soon I hope. Who knows."

"But not today."

"No," he blushed again. "You don't look like you feel okay."

"Allergies. They mowed the yard earlier and it's getting me."

"Are you allergic to everything?"

"Seems like it. Grass, flowers, hay, bee stings."

"Hay?" Charley questioned, picking up quickly on the irony in Riley's life.

"Yes, hay. I know. I have to get an allergy shot."

"Why do you have a hay farm?" Charley asked with that unsure tone. The questioning look the celebrity had at trying to figure out all the mysteries of Riley's town covered his face.

"It's just what we've always done," Riley shrugged. "It's what equipment I have." He smiled at Charley's expression, aware he was now on Charley's list to understand. It didn't bother him. He'd questioned his ownership of a hay farm many times before.

He sat the painting in the chair by his desk and turned his attention to Charley when John Strand marched into his office.

"Mayor Halleran!" Strand was saying, but halted once he saw Charley in there as well. "Sorry to interrupt," his tone changing a bit from the strong one before. "I need a moment of your time."

"Alright," Riley said but felt a wave of nerves at the thought of being alone with that man. "Um, thanks again," he said to Charley, dismissing him quickly, more out of concern that Strand would identify Charley as a culprit in his subdivisions' vandalizing.

Charley left but didn't really seem to want to. Riley shut the office's door after him, not really wanting to isolate himself either.

"Mr. Strand," Riley turned to the man, trying to be polite and set the tone for the meeting but he knew he wasn't going to be able to calm the monster before him. He moved to stand at his desk, hoping to gain some respect at least for the position he held there.

"I have been informed that the man responsible for all the shit happening to my neighborhoods is your father."

"Mr. Strand—"

"—Is this part of your plan as well?"

"My father is known for his outlandish rebellion against whatever cause he fancies at the moment. My father and I are also not that close. I leave his consequences up to the law officers and judges."

John glared at him, leaning on Riley's desk as a means to intimidate.

Riley stood his ground, meeting the man's eyes. "If there's something you wish to know further, ask me."

"The damages that have been done to my equipment and houses are quite extensive."

"I'm sure you have insurance."

"My *insurance* demands a criminal prosecution. Now I have evidence of your father's doings. I have evidence of an accomplice. Should that accomplice prove to be you—"

"—I can assure you I am not involved and I don't like you accusing me of such."

"I can assure you, Mr. Halleran, that I don't like the resistance I'm receiving from your father and from you and your council here. Now when your father is arrested, I will prosecute him to the very edges that I am allowed. He has irritated me for almost ten years and I intend to get him for every little bit, financially and physically. He will rot in jail and I will be the owner of your farm. I will own you and your father."

Riley's reaction was instant. "Perhaps you need to look in the mirror at yourself and see your soul burning in Hell for all the wrongs you've committed against the poor people that have bought your homes or allowed your houses to be there. I *will* vote against this rezoning. You will not build anything in my town. I don't care what you have or think you have against my father. He is an annoying, troublesome man but he speaks the truth and there will be a field of support around him and myself."

John Strand eased back from Riley's desk, his face still full of anger but he did move back. "I warn you to reconsider your vote, Halleran. That vote just might be what saves you, your father and your home."

"It won't save my town, though. What is my farm compared to saving that?"

Strand turned on his heel as crisp as a drill sergeant and left Riley's office, slamming the door behind him.

Riley sat down in his chair, letting out a breath of disgust and fear. Strand's threats had been true enough. His dad would rot in jail and he would lose everything. He'd just have to take it one battle at time and see what happened.

He realized then Lana was standing in the doorway, looking in at him like she expected to see him beaten about the face. "Are you okay?"

"Yeah," he replied, giving the simple answer. "Can you find my father for me?"

The next hour had been spent trying to locate his father and a phone call to his lawyer to find out what his next move might be to help his dad and also his town. The arrival of John Strand in Riley's life had been perhaps the worst event to date and he didn't want to accept that the worst hadn't happened yet.

He left the building quickly that night, worrying that Strand might just have someone waiting to beat the shit out of him, but he found someone different waiting for him. Charley leaned against the nose of his car, arms folded, a smile on his face.

"That went badly I bet," he said as Riley approached.

"You have no idea," he said, unlocking his door and tossing his stuff into backseat. He'd left Charley's painting in his office. Charley didn't mention it.

"I was just worried. I wanted to make sure you were okay to drive home."

Riley didn't voice his thought of hitting the highway and just driving away. "Have you been waiting all this time?"

Charley shrugged, as if it was no big deal.

"Did you bail my dad out this last time?"

Charley looked down as if he wasn't comfortable answering that question. "I did."

"If you see him before I do, tell him Strand is after him big time. And he knows there's an accomplice. Don't let this—"

"—It's okay," Charley interrupted, reaching out and rubbing Riley's arm. He smiled, "It's okay. I promise." He looked down at his boots then back at Riley. "I got new tires," he announced as if hoping to erase all of Riley's troubles that night.

"Good."

"I know you've had a bad day."

Riley couldn't look at the caring man before him. "More than you know."

"I'll let you go home. I'll see you later, okay? And don't worry about Daddy-O or me. I've got the *bestest* lawyers," he smiled, holding the smile until Riley smiled too.

Charley moved to his car, twirling his keys on his finger, looking to see who was watching him. He smiled once again at Riley before getting into his car. He started it and backed out. Riley backed out after him but lost him in traffic.

Riley retreated into his DVD of Charley's recent concert that night as a means to escape the hell that was around him. He let himself get lost in the humor that was Charley Claremont, laughing until his side hurt.

He couldn't grasp that the man he'd admired so much on that stage and totally untouchable was in his town and was his friend. It perplexed him and made him feel comforted at the same time.

It was Charley that he wanted to call then, to hear that undeniable voice and prove to his doubting mind that the celebrity Charley was really just a phone call away.

He had the phone in his hand but mentally debated whether to call or not. He started to dial the number then stopped but then dialed it again and let fate take over.

It was Charley's private number he called but he still doubted that Charley would answer. Yet the familiar voice was there, offering a quiet greeting. "Are you okay?" he asked then.

"I am. I was just watching one of your shows and it just blows my mind that you are that person there making me laugh. I guess I had to call to convince myself I wasn't just delusional. I almost didn't call. I didn't know if you'd be sleeping or busy."

"I'm not. I was just sitting here trying to decide whether to call you, actually."

Riley smiled, looking at the television screen where Charley moved about the stage. The sound was muted but Riley knew well enough what Charley was saying.

"So, bad day," Charley said, his way of asking and yet trying to keep the mood light.

"It was from the get-go. And it's not over yet is the worst part. Strand will battle me until he gets his houses built."

"What else happened?"

"Oh, well," Riley stammered but decided to just say it. "Greg cancelled our date for tomorrow like I knew he would."

"I'm sorry."

"No, don't be. I'll get through." He always did. "I guess I was just wondering what you were doing. I'm sorry our meeting got interrupted this afternoon. I still want the story on the painting."

"I promise. One day."

"It might cheer me up," he said, hoping to guilt Charley into the details.

"It might not," Charley sang back in Riley's tone.

"Alright. I'll be patient."

"Am I on your TV right now?"

"Yes, actually."

Charley hummed quickly, no doubt a smile spreading across his face.

"Are you going to tour again?" Riley asked, merely to make conversation and know more about the celebrity that was on his television.

"I should. I have the material. I just don't have the desire."

"If you do tour and come someplace close by, I want to come see the show."

"I will take you to every show."

"No. I don't travel well. I never have."

"Have you ever been out of this county?"

"Yes, smarty. But I was younger and not so mortal."

Charley laughed a bit. He sighed, "I'm starting to think the same way. I'm getting older, craving more of the meaningful existence than the brilliant one. I may have limited time left. I don't want to spend it in customs or layovers or airplanes taking me back to the place I just left. I just want to run naked through the sprinklers," he said, more of his character's tone in his words.

It made Riley laugh. "There's the title of your farewell tour. *Going to Run Naked Through the Sprinklers.*"

"I like it." Charley paused. "Are you really okay? Okay with Greg and all that?"

"I wasn't but Strand's got me too worried to fret over being dumped."

"I won't let Strand touch you or your dad. Don't worry your pretty face. I know mafia."

"He probably does to. Probably runs it."

"Well, don't worry. You fight the good cause. Don't let a cranky jerk ruin your wonderful work."

Riley took a deep breath then slowly let it out. He wished it was as simple as turning the bad things off. "I'll let you go. I just wanted to hear your voice I guess. Remind myself I'm not crazy."

"You're fabulous," Charley said a smile in his voice. "You get some sleep. Don't think about this stuff tonight. Start thinking about it again at eight-oh-one and not a moment before."

"I'll try. Thanks."

Riley hung up the phone and moved about the house turning off the TV and lights, heading to his bedroom. He realized as he did so that it had been years since he'd been able to reach out to another man for support and he liked how he felt. Greg would have told him to get over it. Charley had done so much more than that.

The Last Time

The night of Tom and Olive's anniversary dinner was a stormy night. The heavy rain had Riley cursing his windshield wipers on the drive over and running for Tom's door once he got there.

He'd known Charley wouldn't be there after all. It had been a last minute show issue that had called Charley away that morning. Riley didn't question the details of it, knowing Charley wasn't lying, but seeing Tom's down expression, he wished he'd done more to make Charley stay. Tom seemed just as disappointed about Charley's absence as he was sad about Olive's.

"At least his plane left before the storms hit," Tom said, distant. "He promised to come see me as soon as he got back."

Riley smiled, feeling sad for his friend who must have been looking forward to dining with the celebrity. "He really wanted to come over."

Tom smiled, nodding.

"Are you okay?" he asked Tom, seeing for the first time Tom's age.

"I guess this weather's getting me. I'm really tired."

"We can do this another night."

"Naw. You're here. Let's eat. Maybe I'll perk up." Tom stood up and went to the kitchen where a pot of soup cooked. Riley followed, going to fix them glasses of iced tea while Tom fixed their soup. There was with a comforting familiarity around them as they did so.

The small table was set for three. A bowl of soup was placed at Olive's chair where two roses laid. Tom said Grace, a few words of sweetness directed in Olive's direction, and then they began to eat.

"This was her favorite," Tom said before taking his first spoonful. "I remember the first night she fixed this for me," he said after a few moments, a brightness about him. "We just went through the pantry to see what we had and made do with what we found."

Riley smiled, sharing in the tenderness of the memory, letting Tom experience it again. "I really can't imagine what it feels like to have spent so many years with the same person. Well, with any person, actually, but the same woman all those years."

"She made it easy," Tom smiled. "Made there be no other woman in the world to me."

"You are blessed to have had such a great life together and to have a love so strong that you can feel it even now."

Tom smiled, proud. "You were the son we never had. We wish all the blessings that were in our life to be in yours as well."

"Thank you. I am definitely blessed to know you both," he said, deciding to leave his statement in the present tense in case Tom was thinking Olive was there too.

Riley left Tom's shortly after dinner, letting Tom turn in early for the night. Tom explained his tiredness away as the weather or the busy week but Riley felt it was something more.

It was shortly after he got home that his dad called with news he hadn't been surprised to hear. He'd been arrested and was in Greene County's jail. Would Riley come bail him out?

While he had Russell's assurance he wouldn't be arrested too, Riley walked into Greene County's jail with apprehension. He'd never been arrested, never been in any jail other than Russell's and that one had felt safe. The jail that time intimidated him. Although he was just there to bail out his father, he felt like the guards were watching him like he belonged inside. He expected to be grabbed and frisked at any moment.

Riley paid the bail, knowing he was going to have to ask Tom for the money to cover it.

The ride to his father's house started out silent and thick with tension. There were so many thoughts racing through his mind, Riley decided to keep quiet. He could tap into the temper he'd inherited from his father if he chose to and it wouldn't be pretty. So he stayed quiet.

And the fact that they had arrested Rennick on suspicion of sabotaging Strand's properties was fueling stress that Riley couldn't even begin to think of how to deal with. Strand was a ruthless businessman that he wasn't equipped to do battle against and they both knew it.

After twenty minutes of intense silence, Rennick spoke, "Do you ever think I might be doing the right thing?"

"Right thing?" Riley laughed, then forced himself back into silence. Did his dad not know that he'd been lucky there had been bail set? Strand's threats were coming true.

Several more tense moments passed and then Riley calming stated, "I can't bail you out anymore. I don't have any money. I've had to scrounge every time for your bail."

"I'll get you the money tomorrow morning."

"Really? Where? Where are you just going to pull five thousand from? Counterfeiting too? Do you care at all that Strand is going to hang you?"

Rennick was silent.

"Where do you have money? What about your farm then? Why haven't you helped with that?"

"It's not mine. It's yours."

"Your name is on it, which is probably a bad idea on my part, isn't it. Strand will sue you and get that farm and I'll lose the one place I enjoy being at. I shouldn't expect you to care about that though, huh?"

"You fight to hang onto that place, not me."

Riley shook his head, refusing to look at his dad. "This is it, okay? No more. No more jails. No more protesting. Those days are over. Who's attention are you trying to get anyway?"

"Maybe yours."

Riley shook his head. "This isn't about me. You are a grown man and acting like a teenager."

"Only protesting a wrong that must be righted."

"Do it some other way. I am tired of this. I'm not going to bail you out again. You want my attention, fine, you got it. Now start acting like a proper citizen of my town. How does it look for the mayor's father to be the worst troublemaker?"

"All worried about your reputation, aren't you. Carrying the burden of politics. Ooh, don't let the troublemaker father out. In case you haven't noticed, your town isn't all that perfect."

"I know it's not. But this is ridicules. What are you protesting? Cheap houses?"

"You don't understand because you're becoming one of them."

"One of them? Who? Someone who wants to live a nice life and help others do the same?"

"Someone who's not thinking about the greater good."

Riley let out a sigh, shaking his head. He'd had this argument so many times with his father and it never changed. "Whatever," he gave up. "Just don't call me to bail you out anymore."

Rennick grunted like Riley had forbidden him to remain in the state. "Why are you so angry at me?"

"Why?! You don't know?! I'm angry because you left when mom got sick. You didn't help me take care of her or bury her. You haven't helped me keep that farm or take care of it. You haven't supported me in my job. You wreck havoc in this town and embarrass me. You want to protest, fine. Do it someplace else." Riley said the last sentence and immediately wished he hadn't. They'd never been truly father and son but Riley was used to him always being somewhere near there. The idea of his dad really leaving troubled him, but he didn't say anything more.

"Fine," Rennick said after a few moments, his tone defeated. "All about you isn't it. Ever think of me? What I feel?"

"I don't have to," Riley said, most of his anger calmed with Rennick's tone. "Your feelings are all over town; on buildings, on flag-poles." He waited for his dad to respond but he said nothing. "This is the last time, dad."

"Yes, it is," Rennick said, his tone full of hate.

They didn't speak the rest of the time.

Leftovers From Charley

Suddenly Riley's life seemed to be about absences. Charley had been out of town for a few days. He had called one time but had been so frustrated and tired he didn't really talk long. He'd returned to town late and planned on sleeping a long time so Riley hadn't bothered him.

Tom's sadness had seemed to take hold and while Tom had still been there to help out, he just hadn't been himself.

Rennick had been absolutely silent since Riley had dropped him off after their argument. He wouldn't accept Riley's calls and refused to have him go to his court date with him.

And Greg, well, Riley would have expected nothing less from him.

Letting the horses into the grassy lot by the barn, Riley smiled as the youngest pranced past him, causing the herd to speed up their steps a bit. The sounds of their footsteps sent a joy through him. He tried to hang onto the brief moment as long as he could but he moved on to shutting the gates and getting back to work.

He leaned against the rails, watching the horses move and begin to graze. Looking past them, into the distance in Tom's direction, he knew Charley and Tom were having dinner. Although he had been invited, Riley had gracefully declined, wanting Tom to have his dinner with the celebrity. He couldn't help but wonder what they were talking about though.

He turned his focus back to his horses, watching them, awed by their strength and beauty. Scarecrow stepped over to the fence, raising his head to Riley, standing still as Riley petted his nose and neck. "I wish my life could just be about you," he told the horse, mentally tired of thinking about Strand and his father.

Scarecrow nudged him ever so gently then perked his head up high making him turn to see what had their attention. He looked down, feeling the smile come to his face. He wasn't surprised by the visitor headed his way. Charley's Pacifica slowly approached and parked. He left the horses, walking to meet Charley at the car's side.

"Well," Charley said, stepping out of his car, "I can see you had good company for dinner as well."

It took him a moment to figure out what Charley had meant, then realized the moment with Scarecrow and himself had been witnessed. "Oh," he looked back at the horses, finding they'd all moved on, "they're just happy because I fed them."

"How about you? You eaten?"

"Not yet."

"Excellent." Charley moved to the back seat, retrieving two foil-covered bowls. "Leftovers but they'll still be good. Tom said you probably wouldn't have eaten yet and then would just eat crap."

"He's probably right. Thanks. You didn't have to though."

"I know," Charley smiled.

"How was dinner? Tom okay?"

"Dinner was fine. Tom's fine," Charley reported, leaning against his car. "He's still very sassy for his age. I like him. We just talked about his wife and their life together. It was touching, very sweet. Did you not go for a reason?" he dared.

"I just wanted him to be able to talk to you. He was pretty disappointed the other night when you didn't get to be there. He's told me all his stories. I figured he'd rather enjoy just telling you. I'm worried about him. He doesn't seem to be himself."

"He's just worried about you. Thinks of you as a son and he can't figure out how to help you with all this town stuff."

"Oh," Riley looked at the horizon, seeing the sunset beginning to take on bright shades of red. "Well, I'll just say I didn't miss dinner for any real reason. I just didn't want to interfere with Tom's night. I did have a yard to mow and a farm to take care of," he offered, smiling.

"Anything I can do to help?"

"All dressed up and you want to do farm chores?"

Charley smiled at him, his expression telling Riley that he'd do it if Riley asked him to.

"No, I'm almost done, really."

"I'm sorry I missed the dinner the other night," Charley looked down. Riley could see the exhaustion in the man's face then as he started to let his character slide away.

"Don't be. You have responsibilities that have to be handled. And you're back now, so don't worry about it."

"I do, though. I really meant to be there and I always let work steal me away from where I really want to be," he explained, looking at the sunset Riley had noticed earlier. Charley sighed, "I'm sorry about it."

"You're talking to a man who thinks and worries about work all the time so don't worry. I understand. Some things have to be dealt with before it gets worse. It's okay."

Charley smiled, nodding. "Well, I'll get out of here. I just wanted to bring you some food," he said as he opened the driver's door. "I must say I liked the man I saw out there earlier," he nodded in the direction of the barn. "He wasn't thinking about work."

Riley nodded. "I like that man, too. He's around sometimes. Not very often."

"I hope to see him soon then," Charley replied, looking Riley in the eyes.

He could only smile and look away. "Go get some rest, enjoy being away from work yourself."

"I will. Oh, are you going to your dad's court gig tomorrow?"

"He doesn't want me there or so I was told by his girlfriend. He's not taking my calls anymore."

Charley frowned, "I was hoping he'd gotten over it by now."

"He doesn't operate that way. We can go years without speaking."

"Well I'm going. I'll let you know what happened."

"Thanks. I really hopes it goes okay."

"Me, too." Charley hesitated like there was something more he wanted to say and then moved on, getting in the car and shutting the door. He started the engine then rolled the window down. "Go eat dinner before it gets cold. Have sweet dreams."

Riley

Riley couldn't stop his smile, hit with a wave of disbelief that Charley Claremont was actually sitting in his driveway. "Sweet dreams to you as well," he replied, loving Charley's playfulness.

He watched Charley back up and then drive away, offering one more wave before he called the dogs too him and they headed inside for dinner.

Riley's Bad Night

The day was spent with an anxiety that Riley didn't like and didn't want to share with anyone. He spent it watching the clock, thinking about what his dad was doing, wondering if he was at the courthouse, were they beginning the proceedings, was he making it worse?

Deep down inside, he didn't really expect to learn anything other than his dad had been whisked away to prison. Going against Jonathon Strand seemed like a battle not even the richest man with a whole team of lawyers could win.

So when he saw it was Charley calling, he took a deep breath and answered.

"I have good news," Charley sang.

"Really?" Riley asked, not believing it to be possible.

"The judge threw your dad's case out."

"Really?" he asked, sitting up. "Really?"

"You should have seen him. He was spectacular. He had all his previous cases from Sleeper, showing a history of minor incidences, nothing in the league of what he was charged with in Strand's realm, which he was quick to continually point out there was no evidence. The best part was," Charley continued, speaking quickly with excitement, "he blew Strand's charges away by pointing out that Strand was involved in a zoning request with Sleeper, in which his son was the mayor and how it would seem that Strand was trying to force that vote by accusing a troublemaking, true, relative of such severe charges. He was brilliant."

"You saw him in his arena," Riley smiled, memories of watching his dad practice his cases back in their happier days of a family home. "He was meant to be in that courtroom." There was some pride in Riley's tone and he let it be there.

"Your dad is proud of you, actually, standing up to Strand like you did the other day."

"How'd he know about that?"

"I might have mentioned it."

"How do you know what happened?" Riley asked, curious.

"I ran into your secretary the next day, actually."

"Actually," Riley sighed but didn't feel bad about them having talked. "A man of many sources, huh?"

"I am. But I know that your dad is going to be as stubborn as he always is so I wanted you to know what happened."

"Thank you. I'm glad you were there. I'm glad he's okay."

"You should call him."

"I have called him. I was told he didn't want to talk to me."

"Maybe keep trying."

"I've got a lot to do. He can call me."

Charley was quiet to that. "I do think I should fix you dinner one night."

He wasn't sure whether to agree or not. Was it a date or was it just a friendly gesture?

"I'll let you get to work. I'll call you later."

"Okay. Thanks, again."

"Anytime."

But his good feeling about his dad's freedom and Charley's calling was quickly wiped away not long after. Riley became defensive the moment he was called that afternoon. Danny Walters was calling a meeting of the council that night. He didn't say what the reason was, but Riley knew. If there was anyone that he would consider an enemy, Danny Walters was it. The rest of his afternoon was full of his mental worries at what the reason was and what verbal attack was he about to face, *if* it ended there and didn't end with his job being in jeopardy.

Most of the council members were already in the conference room when Riley walked in. He couldn't tell what the first part was about, but he walked in to hear Jerry Kinders exclaim, "We're liberal. Hell, our mayor is a homosexual." He was speaking in a strong, angry tone until he spotted Riley and his steam ran out on the last word.

He surveyed the room. Danny wasn't there yet. "What's up?"

"This Strand," Annette said. "He's causing quite a stir around here."

"What's he done now?"

"He keeps promising to make this a liberal, lively town," Charles Abrahams spoke up. "Bring us out of this conservative dying shell." Charles' tone sounded like he was upset at Strand's actions but at the same time they seemed accusing to Riley, like what did he have to promise them?

Danny's entrance into the room silenced them all. Some began to fidget, others merely looked down. Everyone was uncomfortable being there and Riley was sure he knew why. They were all plotting against him. He was called to that room with no allies.

He could get the town to run you off. Even your friends will turn against you.

Riley took his usual chair but hesitated on calling the meeting to order. Danny had actually called the meeting but Riley didn't feel good about giving him the control that night. "So," he said, "you called this meeting?" he asked, bypassing all the procedure and not giving into the power play.

"I felt we needed more time to discuss this subdivision issue before we vote next week. Some of us don't feel too comfortable with our expected votes just yet."

Some of us. "Expected votes?"

"You'll no doubt vote against it, once again voting against something that could revive this town."

"I'm doing what I feel is best for the town," he tried to explain calmly and not be affected by the sting of Danny's words.

"Are you? In the long run, is this best? You kept out the logging company and the chain store. Now you're going to deny people housing?"

Riley smiled at the undisguised attack. "I'm not against housing. I'm not against a subdivision. I *am* against cheaply built, possibly future eyesores of a subdivision done by a man so wealthy he cares only about money and not the people he says he cares for. I simply want to protect that land from being destroyed for a bunch of cookie-cutter homes we're all going to hate. And I don't expect any of you to vote any differently than you think you should. That is why there is a council, not just one man running the show. You each have a vote. Whichever vote wins is what we do." That statement seemed to take some of the wind out of Danny's sail.

"I just have to say," Danny said, finding his stance again, "that this town is eventually going to run out of options for surviving.

We're going broke as it is. Strand could be the saving grace for this town and if you vote against this, I feel the need to start the motion to have you ousted."

Riley had expected to hear those words but even when he did, it affected him. The man sitting across the table from him stared at him, ready to start a war, totally unaffected by the fact that he would take everything from Riley that meant anything to him. "Fine," Riley nodded, deciding it was best to not get upset. "You start your motion." Riley quickly looked at the other council members around him, careful not to judge which side they were on. "If that is it for tonight, I'm sure we all are ready to go home. We'll meet Tuesday and vote. You do whatever you feel you have to." He stood, not going to sit in there and face attacks possibly from the whole council. "All of you, vote however you feel is right."

Riley chose to drive around for awhile to try to calm down. All he discovered was that traffic was as irritating as the memory of a smug Walters' tone. When he finally decided he'd just leave his fate up to the town and the council, he headed for home. If he did get ousted as mayor, perhaps he'd just join his dad in being trouble for the new mayor, Daniel Walters, as that was no doubt Danny's plan.

The car that was parked in his driveway didn't help him feel better, only added a new layer of turmoil. Greg's vehicle announced his presence, making Riley wonder if he was there to break-up in person or if all of Riley's suspicions had just been silly worry. The way his night was going, he knew which one was true.

Greg's expression as Riley stepped inside spoke volumes of how their night was going to go. He offered no smile, only a glare. "You're late."

"I had a meeting."

"You could have called."

Riley was shocked by his anger in that statement. "I didn't know you were here. I didn't know you were coming."

Greg glared at him as if unable to come up with a response to that but still wanting it to be Riley's fault. "I fixed dinner but it's all ruined now," he reported, moving back into the kitchen and setting a few more dishes in the sink. "I was just getting ready to leave."

"Sorry," he shrugged. "I didn't know. I had to go to a meeting and face the council that will probably vote to have me impeached next week," he reported, hoping for some sympathy from Greg but the words didn't seem to touch him. Greg seemed oblivious to his troubles, stuck in his own anger at Riley not being there.

He followed Greg into the bedroom, unsure what mood Greg was in. "I'm here now," he said. "Will you stay?"

"I need to leave soon," Greg replied, picking up his bag, not looking at him.

"Well, sorry." He didn't know how many times he had to say he didn't know Greg was coming out before that fact would sink through Greg's anger. He waited for some kind of reaction from Greg to judge what would happen next. He wasn't sure whether to keep talking or whether to merely wait for Greg to lead the next moments. The longer Riley waited in that silent room, the more he just wanted to go to bed and sleep and let Greg be angry or not and just let the world go away if it wanted to.

Greg still silent, Riley left the bedroom and went back to the kitchen. He meant to sneak a peek at whatever had been cooked and they could have a reheated dinner, but he found all the pans and food in the sink. Greg had dumped them in anger, he understood that. "Fine," he sighed.

Turning, he found Greg standing in the hall. "Come to bed," he said, Riley knowing what he had in mind.

"Greg, I'm tired. I've had a bad night."

"Come to bed," he said, no hint of anger in his words but Riley understood he wasn't going to be able to say no.

Their move to the bed was robotic, cold. The lights were off in the bedroom as Riley walked in. Greg undressed and laid on the bed. Riley undressed himself, trying to find some area in his mind that could push out all his troubles for some sort of arousing fantasy that could get him in the mood quickly, but nothing worked. He simply didn't want to have sex with the man that was upset at him over something he knew nothing about. He wanted that man to hold him and tell him he wasn't going to lose his job or his lover, that Greg was going to love him forever.

He got on the bed beside Greg and leaned down to kiss his strong stomach. He moved lower, taking him in his mouth, hoping that would be the quickest way to end the night.

Charley's Magic for Riley

The doorbell was ringing and ringing. Waking slowly from his dream, Riley sorta thought it had been ringing for a while. *Who could possibly be here this early?*

The ringing was replaced with knocks on the door and then a few knocks on the windows, like whoever was knocking was looking inside for signs of life.

Riley just wanted to sleep but the knocking went back to the door bell ringing. With an angry sigh, he quickly left the bed and searched out his clothes from the night before. He quickly dressed, trying to be presentable enough as he hurried to the door. Fighting the urge to scream at whoever was there, his frustration at being disturbed doubled and failed him the instant he saw Charley standing at the door.

"Oh," he sighed, finding Charley at the door, all sunshine and smiles.

"I brought you the cookies," he said, moving into the living room. "I'm sorry to hound you about it but I couldn't leave them out there because they'd melt." He turned and winced as he looked upon Riley. "Are you hungover?"

"I'm tired," he mumbled. "I'm sorry. I forgot you were coming over. I had a late night."

"Wasn't good, I would guess."

"Thanks for these," Riley said, taking the bundle of cookies from him, leaving the door open, "but I'm not feeling social, okay? I'd like to be alone."

"I don't think you should be alone," Charley said, concern lacing his tone. "Let me fix you something to eat. You're more than tired, I'd say. Let me cook for you. You go back to bed. I'll wake you when it's ready, then I'll go quietly."

"Not necessary."

"It is." Charley moved into the kitchen, leaving Riley alone in the living room with his reasons why Charley should just leave.

He gave in, shutting the door. He went to the kitchen, sitting the cookies down, seeing Charley searching the fridge. "I don't have much."

"I see that. Just like your dad, huh? Never eat but at the café."

"I don't have time," Riley offered a soft-spoken excuse, his eyes going reactively to the collection of dirty dishes Greg had left from dinner.

Charley gave them a glance as well but said nothing. "Go to bed. It'll be a bit."

"I can't sleep with someone in my house," Riley smiled, another soft-spoken excuse that was normally true but that morning he didn't feel like being awake.

"Go," Charley said, with a motherly tone.

He decided not to fight it and returned to his bedroom. He was a bit nervous being alone with Charley but his worries were instantly gone as he drifted to sleep just after his head hit the pillow.

It was almost an hour later when he heard someone calling his name. It came back to him quickly who was there. Charley stood in the doorway of his room, not daring to step into the room, no threat to him. "It's ready to eat if you want."

"Okay," he mumbled.

Charley left as Riley sat up. He made himself leave the bed and quickly made himself more presentable. He was still tired but he could smell the food and that was more tempting than more troubled sleep.

Charley had a cute, embarrassed smile to him as Riley joined him in the kitchen. "I have to confess," he said, nervously wringing his hands as if his way to keep himself from talking with them, "I burned some of it. I mean, it's the first time that's happened since, God, since I was in school with Chef Batolie breathing down my neck. Please don't tell anyone, okay? It'll ruin my reputation."

"I won't tell. It smells good anyway. Looks great." He scanned the stove top quickly but gave up identifying any of the fancy dishes Charley had presented to him.

"Thanks," Charley smiled, looking down, his blush becoming more girlish. "I'm impressed, too," he nodded. "I wasn't expecting much to cook with but you have some top-quality stuff here."

Riley shrugged off the compliment. "I like to cook. I just don't have time."

"Well, I'm impressed."

He looked at his kitchen, aware that Charley had not only cooked, but cleaned up everything, including Greg's disaster from the night before.

They fixed their plates and then moved to the dining room. Riley sat at the end while Charley sat next to him. They ate and shared small talk for a few minutes before Charley turned it in a serious direction.

"I have a confession to make. I snooped a bit," he smiled. "I get nosy when I'm nervous and I saw you had a pile of mail by the phone."

"Yeah?" Riley said nonchalantly, hoping to drop the subject.

"I read it," he said, biting his lip like he expected Riley to become furious.

Riley looked at him, nodding. "And?"

"It's a lot of late bills, Rile. Are you having troubles?"

"I've always had trouble. It's nothing for you to worry about." He loaded his fork up and took a bite, not looking at his guest any more.

"Can I give you some money?"

"No!"

"I just want to help."

"Why? So I'll feel obligated to sleep with you?" The subject of his money was making him defensive. He knew that but didn't change his tone any.

"No. Only to help out. I have money, Rile. I have so much money I can't tell you how much. Let me help you."

It echoed Greg's words. Money was how he could help out there. "No."

"Okay," he said, "but if you change your mind, let me know."

"I won't."

"Your dad's right. You get your pride from him."

"That's probably all I got from him," he said under his breath, sure that he had ruined the sweet morning like he had ruined the night before. He let out a deep breath, looking at Charley.

"I'm sorry. I am not in a good mood and I can't pretend to be in one."

"I know. I almost had you in one though," he smiled.

They fell silent again, eating.

"Rie, I want to ask about the dishes and whatever happened last night, but I won't."

"Okay," he agreed, ending that conversation, knowing that wasn't what Charley had been leading up to. Charley just nodded and let it go.

A few moments passed quietly, then Charley started again. "I just feel there's so much unhappiness about you and I want to just wash that away."

"I doubt that's possible, really." He sighed. "I have my bad moments but I have lots of good ones too. I just happen to be in a bad moment, okay?"

"You care about this town, your family, your farm, but what about your soul, your heart? You've lost yourself, Riley. You're scattered in tiny bits across this town. So many fights going you can't fight them all."

"I have a lot of responsibility. Perhaps you don't have that same pressure," he said, feeling angry at Charley's lecture when Charley knew more about his troubles than anyone.

Charley thought and then nodded. "True. But you have this pressure and nothing else. Your life is full of fights for other people that aren't going to remember you when they get what they want. Full of being at other people's mercy when they want to see you."

Riley looked down, knowing he meant Greg. "And you're different? We have sex tonight, you'll remember me tomorrow. You'll be fine with settling in a hick town that can't even tell you were Hollywood is? You'll still want to have me around. You get what you want from me, you'll be different than all these other people you think are using me?"

"Yes, I'll be different," he nodded, "and you'll be different too," he added in a seductive tone. "You'll see through people's lies and cut the shit out of your life. You'll be free to live like you want to. You and I will move through the future in love and ecstasy."

Riley stopped his laugh, turning away.

"You need to see how unhappy you are. There's such a sadness around you aliens in space can see it."

He looked at Charley, hoping not too much of his emotions showed on his face. Charley wasn't telling him anything he didn't already know. He couldn't deny it, he just simply didn't want to talk about it. "So what do you suggest? I have sex with you and all my troubles will go away? Strand won't ruin my life or my town? People will like me once again? Bills pay themselves?"

Charley looked away. "I want that," he quickly said, meeting Riley's eyes, "to be with you. But that's not why I'm here. I'm sorry I mentioned anything," he said, taking his plate and leaving the room, headed to the kitchen.

Riley took his plate and followed. "You just have no idea what I'm really going through. You're watching my life but not living it."

"I know. I'm sorry. I meant to cheer you up and I'm just raining on you even more. I apologize," he said, looking almost as if he was going to cry. "I just know you're going through a lot and I want to make it better. Sorry. I'll clean up in here and leave you with my cookies of happiness and I won't mention anything more."

Riley felt like dirt. "Charley, it's not that. I'm in a bad mood and I've been attacked by so many people lately and I just react that way. My paranoia thinks that Strand has gotten to you and you're trying to convince me to leave this town. I'm sorry I complicated that. Really, I'm sorry."

Charley nodded, still looking sad. "Do you want me to leave?"

"No." He sighed, trying to force away all the bad feelings he had about himself that morning. "No, I don't want you to leave. I'm sorry."

Riley went to sit on the porch and lose himself in watching the wind blow the trees while Charley quickly cleaned up and then joined him, sitting on the step but turned to face Riley. Charley's mood had seemed to lift. They sat in silence a moment, both watching the dance of the trees.

"This is where I retreat to," he explained to Charley then. "No matter how I feel, I can watch the trees move and bend and listen to the leaves and I feel better."

"It's perfect," he smiled.

They watched the trees a few moments more then Charley spoke. "One reason I wanted to see you today is I'm leaving tonight."

The words made Riley look down. "Oh."

"I should be back Wednesday, maybe Thursday. I have a show to film, a job to do."

Riley smiled. He hadn't really thought about Charley having a *job*. "I don't know how you travel like that, why you work so much when you don't have to."

"I enjoy it. I enjoy people. Well, I did."

"People," Riley smiled at him. "Let's talk about people. What are you doing to the people of this town?"

"I have no idea what you mean," he said, obviously lying.

"I mean Beatrice and Olivia shopping together. Jacob Cordray was almost civil to me the other day and he talks to no one. Ole Teddy at the café admitted to knitting his own socks. What is this magic you're working on this town?"

"Because you need some?" Charley asked, not threatening with his tone.

Riley's smile began to fade and he nodded. "I do."

"I just listen. These people all want the same thing: validation from a friend."

It made Riley smile again. A friend, that was what he wanted.

"I have time to listen," Charley offered.

Riley took a deep breath and slowly let it out. "Should we go get the cookies?"

"Naw. Those are just for you."

He let his attention fall once more on the trees and was overwhelmed by what troubled him the most. "I'm losing everything," he confessed. "I'm losing Greg. Been losing him for a while even though he's not really here for me to lose. Greg loves me if it's just us but couldn't ever be mine around others. He's always hiding who he is, always afraid someone is going to find out. And it's okay. It's done. I know that. I'd just like for Greg to know he missed out on something. I just want the satisfaction that he regrets not loving me.

"I'm losing the farm. I can't hardly pay the bills on a good day and I don't remember what a good day is. If Strand gets his way, he'll have me kicked out of here before I have time to even blink.

"I'm losing my job. By not letting in all this destructive stuff and what some think is great stuff, they think I'm not doing right by the town. There was the threat of voting to impeach me last night so I'll lose that no doubt."

"I didn't know that."

He nodded. "If that happens then I lose my town 'cos I can't remain here and watch it destroyed, all the trees pushed down for asphalt and horrible houses. I'll have to move." He looked at Charley then, offering a slight smile. "I'm losing it all but at the same time, a part of me wants to lose this all, to start over and not care about these problems anymore."

"I don't think you could leave. This seems to be where you belong. You are the defender and the protector of this town. I don't think they'll turn on you."

"What if they do? What if Strand gets to put his subdivision in? I don't think I can fight for my town anymore. I'm beat," he softly confessed. He sighed then added, "But I'm not capable of giving up. What do I do? Ride through town naked on horseback?"

"Your dad would be proud to help you. He's very proud of you, Rie. Don't think he isn't. He doesn't do what he does to get at you."

"It seems like that most of the time. I try to get him to help me, not work against me."

"He thinks he is helping you."

"He's helping the ulcers form. Doesn't matter. Strand is out to get him, and his accomplice, and will sue my dad for all the damages which will award him this farm and my dad's soul, maybe even mine and part of yours."

Charley looked away, affected by Riley's statement. He sat up, stretching, biting at his lips like he was gathering unpleasant thoughts to speak. "I sorta wish I had met you, say, ten years ago, when life hadn't beaten you up like this and when life hadn't beaten me up. We could just sit and watch the trees dance and not be hiding from our troubles."

"What are you hiding from?"

Charley smiled, sighing. "Right now, I'm hiding from that world out there where an airplane waits to fly me who knows how many states away to become this pretentious queen kissing celebrity asses when all I want to do is sit here and eat cookies and wait for the rain to move in."

Riley smiled at him, aware the words spoken were more than just a rant about his job but a pure expression of love for him. He felt unworthy of it and wasn't sure what to say. "I'm going through this with Greg right now. I don't want to lead you on or anything."

"You're not. I just want you to know that I do honestly want to get to know you. I'm sorry I made such a spectacle of it when I moved here but that was still the pretentious queen of me. I hadn't had time to get out of character yet," he paused. "For the first time, I don't want to get on that plane. In all my travels and all the places I've been, with all my friends and lovers, I never felt like I was *leaving* anything," he said, his eyes filling with tears. He looked away, trying to deny them, to smile them away. He quickly wiped his eye, shaking his head. "Sorry. I'm having separation anxiety," he smiled.

"I can't really promise that I'm anything worth feeling that over."

"I know and I ask nothing. I just wanted to be honest. I just wanted to say good-bye and make sure you were in a good place for me to leave you alone," he smiled.

He smiled back, aware that he was feeling a little sad himself, knowing Charley wasn't going to be in town for a while. "Well, at least I know my dad won't be getting you arrested."

Charley nodded, not speaking like it would have pushed him into tears again.

Their moment was interrupted by the sound of an old truck coming down the drive. It backfired once after the engine shut off.

"That's Tom," Riley reported, the truck's sound unmistakable.

Charley wiped his eyes once real quick as they turned to wait for Tom's appearance at the side of the house.

Tom smiled when he saw the two of them. He nodded at Charley, "Miss Claremont, it's a surprise to see you here," he said, looking at Riley quickly then moving on past them. He took a seat next to Riley.

"I just had to deliver some cookies to Mr. Depressed here."

"I heard about the meeting last night," Tom looked at Riley, concern in his eyes. "The whole town's talking about Walter's threat."

Riley looked out at the trees, hoping their dance would whisk him magically away from his troubles there. "I can't do anything to stop it."

"I don't think the town will go for it. You've helped too many people out there for them to just turn on you."

"People do that," he sighed, looking at Tom then down at the yard he needed to mow. He would have to leave if it happened, he thought. He couldn't show his face in town, afraid any one of them would verbally (or worse) attack him. Easily outnumbered, Riley's paranoia flared up strong. All that would be on his side were the old man and the weird celebrity that the town would probably turn on as well, no matter what magic had already been worked.

They fell into an uneasy quiet. Riley felt his two guests were just being cautious around him, afraid that he would freak out or break down. His job was in jeopardy as was his future. His friends didn't really know how to help him with that and Riley honestly didn't know of anything that would help him feel better right then. He was consumed once again with his feeling of losing everything and that wasn't what he wanted.

"So," Tom spoke up, "anything good to eat here?"

"There's some leftovers in the refrigerator," Charley reported. "Enough for a good full lunch."

"Sounds perfect."

Their small talk died away again. It had been all they were able to maintain and keep the focus off Riley.

"So you'll be gone until Thursday?" he asked Charley, making himself join them and not remain in his internal hell of fear and worry.

"I'll try to get back as soon as I can."

Riley nodded, feeling more consumed by the nausea in him as if Charley's leaving was tearing down all the protective fields around him.

Charley stood up, dusting off his pants, fidgeting. "I should go. I *am* going."

"Well, thanks for listening and for the cookies and for breakfast," he said as he walked with him to the car. "Thank you. I'm sorry for my mood earlier. I didn't mean to be hateful to you. You've been the only one there for me besides Tom."

"You're welcome. No apology needed. You're fine." They stood at the car in an awkward moment. "I feel horrible leaving you when you're obviously full of all these problems."

Riley smiled, looking down at his feet. "I really wish you could take all this away. I'm starting to think I can't take it."

"Just stay in the moment," he offered, reaching over and petting Riley's upper arm. "You'll be okay. Worry gets you nothing. Right now you have the sunshine and the trees and a good friend there," nodding towards Tom's place on the porch.

That much was true but there was still another wall hitting him of Charley's leaving and it bothered him. It would have been a nice day for Charley and him to just visit and talk and ease each other's troubles.

But Charley had a plane waiting and a job and Riley couldn't offer him anything to compete with that.

At least, he didn't think he could.

He wasn't sure what to say or do then. Handshake? Hug? "I'll see you when you get back then."

Charley smiled, nodding.

Riley and Tom saddled up two horses and headed out into the field. It was a pleasant ride for them, one they usually took if the weather was just right. That afternoon, both men seemed to be in their own thoughts. Riley guessed Tom was feeling sad about Olive being gone and perhaps planning how they were going to do hay that year and perhaps a part of his silence was merely out of respect for Riley and all his troubles.

Whatever their reasons, the ride was quiet but still comfortable.

It was only once they came to Widow Kelley's farm that their moods became more of one. That farm covered the horizon with rolling hills and tall, strong trees. Amongst its beauty sat a little farmhouse and barn where Patricia Kelley lived out her remaining days.

The farm was one of the largest in the county. When her loan went into default earlier that spring, Jonathon Strand had been the first in line of those wishing to buy it. With some amount of luck, Pat Kelley had managed to hang on to her home so far but her days and money were running out. It was only a matter of time before Strand got his hands on that land and with the re-zoning he was fighting for, there would be nothing left of the house, barn and fields. There would only be houses: Strand's houses.

Riley looked over the land, feeling he'd let it down. He wasn't able to stop the coming destruction. He couldn't save her farm or his town. He felt his heart breaking as he looked over the majestic beauty before him.

Pat Kelley was like a grandma to that town, never hurting a thing, always giving more than she had. Her husband had died years ago and she'd fought like hell to keep that farm going. She'd been a spitfire of a woman and would have done anything for anyone. And when she needed help, they'd failed to be there for her. Little by little she'd been forced to sell the equipment and livestock and admit defeat to an unfriendly economy that her fixed income couldn't live in.

Riley had other attachments to that farm than just respect for the woman fighting to save it. Her son Brent had been his first lover. They had done it in the barn. He'd since died too. Widow Kelley had lost everything in her life except her home and she was about to lose the place where she'd raised her children and buried her husband and son.

"There's always hope for a miracle," Tom sighed, as if he could read Riley's mind.

"That's *all* we have to hope for," he replied, knowing all his conventional methods had failed. It was going to take a miracle to save everything he loved about his town.

They turned the horses and headed back home. It was only then Riley felt like talking.

"My dad says I hang on to old things."

Tom nodded. "I suppose he might speak the truth: the farm, your truck, me."

"Well, aren't you suppose to play the cards you're dealt? I just get a new farm and friends all the time and feel better about myself?"

"No," Tom shook his head. "You hang on because these make you happy. Hard work isn't for nothing. You like your farm?"

"Yes."

"Your truck?"

"Yes."

"Me?"

"Tom, I love you."

"And Greg?"

Riley realized his answer had been too slow. He hadn't really been grouping Greg into that but after a moment's thought he felt it was appropriate. "Didn't you and Olive have hard times?"

"Sure. But we were together. It was *our* marriage, *our* argument. With Greg, you're separate. *You're* feeling this. *You're* trying to make it work. It's not the same."

"So what do I do?"

Tom was quiet a moment then spoke. "Greg loves you, he does. Know the moment I knew he loved you? That day we had haying and he wanted you to go to that show. He showed up here unannounced and helped us."

"Yeah."

"He loves you. He's just worried about unimportant things, afraid of the public reaction. It's not you. It's all *them* out there. He could come around. He could prove himself."

"And if he doesn't?"

Tom rubbed his chin then continued. "I don't think Greg will ever be fully yours. I know you don't want to hear that but it's what I think. He hasn't moved to sweep you up yet and I don't think he will. And if it continues this way, he'll only treat you worse 'cos he'll resent you and resent having to hide."

"So you think I should go out with Charley, who is the exact opposite of Greg."

"Well," Tom smiled, "perhaps. Date, don't have to marry. Charley has another side too. He's not all show. With you, he's pretty normal. If what I saw on the porch this morning is any indication of what should happen, then you should marry Charley."

"What you saw?" Riley scoffed. "What's that?"

"You two were just comfortable together. You fit together."

"You like him, that's all."

"No. I like *you* around him," Tom leaned in to Riley as he spoke then moved back. "If you'd let yourself, you'd have fun with him. You work so hard and take care of so much and so many people. Take care of yourself for a change. Have fun. That's what's missing with you and Greg. You may have love and sex, but you don't have fun."

Tom's gaze got distant, a smile coming to his lips. "Olive and I used to have fun. We'd go skinny dipping in Ole Porter's creek."

"Wow. That sounds fun," Riley said sarcastically.

"Ever skinny dip?"

"No. My luck I'd get leeches in all the wrong places." They laughed but Riley's heart was quickly full of Greg once more. "I just wish I could make him see it's okay to be with me." He felt a huge sadness take him then. "You know, though, I don't think

I'll ever see Greg again. He's chosen his life and it wasn't with me."

"I'm sorry, kid. I know that hurts."

Riley let his mind swim through all the emotions attached with knowing he was single again and the man he'd loved would never be his. "I just don't like being alone, Tom. I want to have that relationship like you had with Olive. I want to know someone is there for me."

Tom nodded, his own sadness to him. "Well, kid, you'll always have me."

Tuesday

Riley hid in his office most of that Monday, worried about an awkward hallway meeting with one of the council members. He'd started his morning looking at his office and trying to decide if he felt a change coming his way or if he would still be in that office for some time. Giving up on predicting his future, he called Kate Howell at the bank, hoping to issue some winning miraculous argument for them to stop pursuing Widow Kelley's farm. All he was told was the farm was only valuable for its real estate, not like the risk they were taking on the bankrupt factory that promised jobs and loans. The farm promised no return other than at its sale.

At lunch he retreated to his truck and sat on the square eating his lunch, looking at his town. Most of the stores were in need of repair in some fashion. Several of the stores sat vacant and had been so for some time. The buildings were dated like he could easily step back in time except for their age showing in the run-down and faded appearance they all held.

His town was dying, he knew that. There was no money to help what few businesses struggled through clean up their buildings. There was not enough traffic on the square to attract new businesses. Perhaps he should have concentrated harder on revitalizing the square instead of getting the big-business factory to pull in. Perhaps his outlook for that town was just as dated as the buildings and it was time for a new leader to pull them through.

His cell phone began to ring at that thought. He wouldn't have answered it but he knew the number displayed was Charley's. He answered, hoping he was hiding all the sadness and worry that filled him.

They exchanged small talk for a bit. Charley was in California, working, back in his old life, but he would be back there Wednesday afternoon. He wanted to know how Riley's day was going which he didn't answer too truthfully.

"What I really wanted to tell you is this," Charley said. "I wasn't sure I'd get a chance to call you tomorrow so I'm calling now. This is my wisdom. You know how they say the best gift to give is something that you would want to receive yourself? Well, I think the best vote you can give tomorrow night is what you think is best for the town. It is *your* town, Riley. You are the defender and the leader. You know what you want to happen."

"Thank you. I needed that."

The morning light was filling the bedroom. Sunshine was warming Riley's skin. He was kissing someone, could feel the weight of the man roll onto him. The man's hands were holding his head to the kiss. The kiss was foreign, nice. Riley ran his hands down the man's back. He didn't open his eyes to see his lover, merely enjoyed the kissing, the love. His world was at peace. His mind thought of nothing but making love. His body felt nothing but pleasure from the touches and kisses of his lover.

Riley was completely his…

The phone ringing was what stopped his dream. Riley opened his eyes, startled, and then shut them again, disappointed to find himself alone. The dream was merely a dream. Without having seen his lover's face, there was a feeling to him it had been Charley making love to him. He didn't let the pleasure of the dream fade away too quickly, no matter who his lover had been. There had been pure love felt in his dream, something that his reality lacked. He wanted to hang on to that feeling.

And then his alarm went off and all the dread of knowing it was Tuesday morning and the crucial meeting that night washed all his pleasurable feelings away.

He moved through his day as usual, sometimes debating what his choice would be and then sometimes positive he knew what to do. He knew he'd be looking into Strand's eyes that night as the vote was cast. There would be no denying who were enemies in the war. He'd just have to see it through until the end, that was all he could do. And if he was impeached, he was impeached. He'd have time to make his hay then and not worry about everyone else for a change.

The council chambers filled up quickly, making Riley feel a bit unnerved at the turnout. He was sure that room was full of Strand supporters. He was surrounded. Even Annette seemed to avoid looking at him like she knew she was about to hurt him.

Riley desperately wanted to look out and see either his dad's face or Charley's but they weren't there. He was alone that night.

The smaller issues were cleared up quickly and then the zoning issue was the focus. It went up for vote quickly, Riley not wanting the meeting to get out of hand with more discussion for or against it. They all knew the issue and the consequences.

Strand sat smugly back in his seat as the vote began. Riley had been too intent on his disgust at the man's presence that he wasn't really sure he'd heard the first three votes were against changing the zoning. But as Strand's stature began to slide, Riley realized that soon there were eight votes against and only two for it. His vote was going to be nine and it was done.

Strand nodded at Riley, not showing his upset and respecting his victory that time. But they both knew Widow Kelley's farm was still out there as was the threat of prosecution of Rennick. He'd lost one fight, but there was still others to be had.

Annette gave him a hug before they parted ways in the parking lot. "Sorry I was so quiet on this," she said, squeezing him. "I just didn't want to give my position away. We were always on your side." She stepped back. "Sometimes I just think it's better to let your enemies show themselves and take care of them."

"Thank you. I was worried, you know that."

"I know. I'm sorry. I'll make it up to you. Lunch, tomorrow. My treat."

Sleep was all he wanted.

Bundled up just right in bed, the world was perfect. He hadn't felt that comfortable in so long. His job was safe. His town was safe. He had the dream from that morning to let drift through his mind. He knew he just had enough time to note that moment of joy before sleep would claim him. The world was becoming distant and all his troubles were gone, even the sound of the phone ringing.

The sound startled his body more than his mind. He knew his heart was racing from the shock but his mind was still more focused on going to sleep.

It didn't matter how perfect the sleep was going to be, Riley had to answer the phone.

It was in partial sleep that he answered. He recognized the caller's voice as his dad's, but it just didn't sound right.

"Dad?"

"I need to go to the hospital, I think. Will you take me?"

He really wanted to go back to bed. He wanted to just rank this call with the many other calls from his dad wanting something. But something felt different. "Do you need an ambulance?"

"No. No." He didn't sound too sure.

"I'll be there as soon as I can."

"Thank you."

Rennick didn't look bad, but he didn't look himself. He was pale and extremely tired. He hadn't taken anything and it wasn't food poisoning, he assured his son. Riley sped as he drove to the hospital, his instinct telling him that something was wrong despite his mind telling him that he was just being foolish.

The longer they waited for a doctor to come in the more anxious Riley got. He was becoming more and more worried. The Rennick Halleran that laid on the exam table was nothing like the dad he knew. This man was quiet, concentrating on the ceiling tile like it was keeping his pain away. He'd groan every so often making Riley's legs feel weak.

And the moment that everything changed in Riley's life had left him unable to do anything. His dad's pain intensified. A flood of nurses and machines and doctors went to his father.

Riley was asked to step outside the room, not able to see his dad in the mix of hands and coats.

His worry eased a bit as a nun entered the room and his dad's voice rumbled through the hallway, "What the hell is *she* doing here?"

But his dad's voice was strained. The commotion was only getting more active in the little room that Riley couldn't be in. He could only stand in the hall and listen to the sound of his dad's heartbeat and to the orders given and then the doctor's tense voice as he spoke. "Mr. Halleran, you're having a heart attack."

Riley stood before the large window in the waiting room, looking over the city of lights that early morning. He was aware Greg was out there somewhere, probably sleeping in his safe, heterosexual world. One of the planes he saw in the sky might hold Charley that said he was coming back there as soon as he could get a plane. While the skyline was awesome from that view, the city so pretty and simple in its dark morning blanket and very little traffic, Riley watched it feeling alone. He felt so small in that huge hospital and in that dark sky of stars that couldn't be seen for all the city lights below him.

Somewhere deep in the hallways behind him, nurses were getting his father prepped for an angiogram. The doctor didn't expect to find anything good. Tonight hadn't been the first heart attack for Rennick Halleran. He'd been extremely lucky to still been alive.

Riley had plans on spending the night in the waiting room, too exhausted to drive all the way home only to have to drive all the way back in a few hours. He had thought about calling Greg and seeing if he could stay there but he wrote that idea off as soon as he thought it. He needed to be there in case Charley showed up anyway.

But he couldn't pull himself away from the window just yet. All he could think about was what if he'd just blown his dad off and rolled over and gone to sleep.

The Hospital

Charley arrived just before six that morning. He looked like crap, like he had been crying since the moment Riley had called him. His hands were shaking as he fumbled with his glasses. "He is okay?"

"As far as I know. They've been in surgery for awhile. The doc seemed hopeful but my dad's going to have to make a lot of changes if he wants to live much longer. We'll both have to work on him."

"I'll start on him as soon as I see him. I've told him to stop smoking so much and I'll get him to eat better. I will," Charley nodded, sounding secure that his plan was going to save Rennick's life. He wiped his eyes, whispering a quick prayer. Calm once again, he looked at Riley, "You look horrible," Charley stated, making Riley laugh a bit.

"I haven't slept any."

"How'd the meeting go?" Charley asked as they took their seats and got comfortable.

"Fine. It was 9 to 2 against. I shouldn't have been so worried. Strand still has his chance though. And he could fight our decision if he wanted to. But it went a lot better than I thought it would. Thanks for calling me. I needed it."

"I know you did," he said, reaching over and patting Riley's leg. "Man, I had no idea your dad didn't feel good."

"I didn't either. It's just good he called me. If we hadn't been here, I'm not sure he'd have made it."

Charley groaned, quickly wiping a tear. He took a deep breath and blew it out. "I'll be okay. I've got to calm down, especially if I get to see him."

"Well, it may be awhile so you have plenty of time to relax. Want something to drink? I'll go get it."

"Thanks. Vodka on the Rocks," he smiled. "Or a Mountain Dew."

It was almost ten that morning before they were informed of Rennick's condition and then only Riley was allowed to visit him. His dad was sleeping but actually seeing him helped stop some of his fears. He wasn't hooked up to much machinery and seemed comfortable and no longer in pain. He felt like his dad was going to be okay.

Riley headed home soon after that needing to get some sleep. He made it home in an exhausted daze but made it safely. He drank a glass of milk and then went to lay down. He slept fairly lightly, still consumed with the guilt of 'what if' but he did sleep. It was late afternoon when he woke up and made himself get up and head back to the hospital.

It was his decision to stop by Charley's place to check on him that took all the good feelings he had and crush them.

Parked in Charley's driveway was Jonathon Strand's Escalade.

Filled with emotions he could barely distinguish, Riley drove to his father's side, hoping that he wouldn't be faced with Charley again. All sorts of paranoid theories attacked him and he didn't like any of them but he could think of no good reason for Strand to be at Charley's. He felt used and betrayed all anew.

When Charley did arrive at the hospital later that evening, Riley couldn't bring himself to speak to him. While his dad was awake and was allowed visitors and he didn't feel right about leaving him, Riley took the excuse that there were too many visitors and he'd go home for the night. He'd see his dad in the morning.

Rennick seemed to be understanding but Charley was quite aware of Riley's state. The tension between them had been quite obvious from Charley's arrival. Charley probably didn't know why Riley had changed towards him, probably doubted he knew anyway. Riley wasn't concerned with his thoughts, just simply wanted to be away from him. He wasn't going to play games or be played.

Walking away from the hospital to his truck, he questioned himself on how he could have even thought about considering getting to know that man.

He slammed his truck's door then sat still for a moment, trying to calm down. He only wanted to run to the life he'd been so happy with before all this mess, a life with Greg's love and his dad well and a pain-in-the-ass and no Charley.

He dialed Greg's number, not thinking about what he was going to say, just wanting to hear Greg's voice.

Greg answered, his voice low.

"My dad's in the hospital here. I'd just really like to see you tonight."

"I can't tonight. I have company."

Riley sighed, getting the answer he had really expected. "Even just for a bit? I need to see you."

"I can't, Rile," Greg said, his tone more stern.

"I see." The moment was there but Riley couldn't accept it into him. He knew Greg wasn't the best man for him but that didn't make saying good-bye to him any easier. "You can't give me anything," he said, hoping to fumble his way through to a better ending.

"My life is difficult, Rile. I have to think about things, is all."

"There's nothing to think about. You know what you want. Do you care that my dad almost died? Do you care about me or what happened at the meeting yesterday?" He knew Greg didn't care about Charley.

"I do care." The background noise changed on Greg's end from a radio playing to complete silence. He'd moved to more privacy. *Hiding.* "I thought I made that clear the night we…" he stopped.

"We what? Fought? Fucked?" he stopped, seeing it then. "The night we changed positions, you mean. That wasn't you really loving me, it was you leaving me." Riley closed his eyes, aware the strange feelings he'd had about that night had been right.

"I wanted you to know I loved you. I did that for you."

"No you didn't," he said, wanting to add a few choice words after that but he didn't fight that way. "You only meant to lead me on some more so you could just step out of my life and not be faced with having tell me to get lost."

"No," he said, but there wasn't much strength to his word.

Riley was quiet a moment, fighting his tears, not about to get weak on Greg's account.

"Rie, I'm sorry. I don't want to hurt you and I know I do. But I can't do this anymore. You need to find someone that can be what you need. It's not me. I'm sorry."

"I'm sorry too," Riley said and slammed his phone shut. He threw it away from him, only then looking up to see Charley was standing on the curb near him, having witnessed Riley's call.

He started the truck and quickly left, not looking at Charley again for his reaction.

Inside his house, Riley was consumed with the need to throw something, to hurt something as much as he hurt, but he couldn't bring himself to throw anything and he doubted he was capable of hurting anything so he did what he could. He stepped out onto his back deck and sat down on the stairs. He sat outside all night, feeling sorry for himself, feeling alone in the big world. He welcomed the night's cool rain that soaked him, letting his body feel as miserable as his mind and heart.

Rennick's Confession

Early the next morning, Charley called and left a message that he was heading back to California for the day so Riley was free to spend the day with his father. Perhaps when he returned, they could talk about what was bothering Riley, he said with no emotion to his words.

Riley doubted that, not able to think of what he would say to him.

But as he took a shower that morning, he broke down into tears, all the week's events getting to him. Where his anger at Charley had come from he couldn't decide but he did know that he hadn't even bothered to really find out why Strand had been there or tell Charley that was why he was upset. The week had just been too much with too many major changes. Had he reacted that way to force Charley away from him?

He got his dad home and settled that Friday afternoon. Charley didn't return that day and didn't call him. Rennick reported that he was staying over to finish up some projects but would be back in time for the dinner the next day so Riley knew they'd talk. Charley's silence was only directed at him, which he understood.

There was a surreal moment for him as he sat by his dad's bed while they watched ESPN, discussing sports like a real father and son. It was perhaps the first time.

He stayed until after dinner then began to get ready to leave.

It was while Riley gathered up his keys and wallet that his dad called him over to his bed. "I want you to know something," he said as Riley sat by his side, facing him. "I want to explain something to you so you'll understand your troublemaker dad in case I don't wake up tomorrow."

"Don't say that."

"I want you to know, though." Rennick collected his thoughts, then stated, "I act out so much because I can't deal with your mom not being here. I get angry every time I think about how many mothers are taken from their children, the one thing they really live for. Your mom loved nothing else in this world like she loved you."

"I know that."

Rennick nodded. "And why I wasn't there when your mother got sick? I couldn't be. I couldn't see her. I couldn't lose her. She understood that. She didn't want me to see her like that. She was sick, Riley, for longer than you know. I just couldn't do it. She was my heart. I wanted mine to stop beating when hers did but she insisted that I stay here for you. She couldn't be here to take care of you anymore and she didn't want you to be alone." Rennick smiled, shaking his head. "I'm sorry I let you down. Sorry I let her down. I tried. I wanted to be there, but everywhere I looked, I saw her and... I'm sorry."

Riley hugged him, giving their hug a moment before he spoke. "Well, I'm sure she got quite a kick out of you riding that horse through town."

Rennick laughed, sitting back from his son's hug. "She always thought the sight of me naked was pretty funny."

Riley saw his attempt to lighten the mood, "On that note, I'll go."

Dinner at Charley's

There was romantic music playing at Charley's as Riley and Annette stepped inside. Charley was at the door, welcoming his guests inside with smiles and no signs of fatigue from flying and working. He was dressed in a nice shirt and leather pants and heels with his make-up more than what Riley had seen on other days. He was in pure character that night. His attention was on the collection of ladies that gathered around his kitchen for their lesson and evening with Charley Claremont. Riley sat at the bar, watching the action more than participating except for the one time Charley couldn't get a jar open and asked him to.

Charley was as funny and brilliant as his shows and Riley found himself enjoying the evening despite the concerned looks that Charley cast him every so often, as if he'd really wanted to know they were okay instead of the two just pretending to be. Riley hoped that his comfortable interactions with him would let Charley know they were, but their first moment alone, Charley leaned over and asked.

Riley nodded. "I'm sorry about that. I'll explain later."

It seemed to be enough for Charley. He seemed to erase all his worry and countless hours of having tried to figure out what he'd done that made Riley so mad.

As they moved through dinner, Charley focused on the group of women, Riley discovered he'd stepped into the role of the boyfriend there and he didn't mind it. Whatever the women thought didn't bother him. He was just enjoying the fancy house decorated with Charley's taste for beautiful, practical things with a mix of his own career in the midst. The music was adding to the mood there, the words in Spanish but he liked it just the same. There was a cool breeze blowing through and the wine he sipped in the classy yet delicate glass was better than any he'd ever had and no doubt a lot more expensive. He moved through the living room looking at the art and collection of music, aware that if it had just been the two of them there that night, he could have easily fallen under the celebrity's spell and ended up in his bed.

Charley's dinner was a success, nothing burned or ruined which Riley had worried he might cause. Dinner passed with more joking and laughing and the small group there becoming good friends.

As the evening came to an end, he knew he had to leave when Annette left or he'd be walking home, but he wanted to talk to Charley. Annette just gave him a knowing smile and said to take his time. He left her walking through the living room on the same path he'd taken earlier while he waited for dinner.

All the guests gone but them two, Charley offered him a real smile, letting Charley Claremont retire for the evening. "I was hoping to talk to you before this but I got in late."

"It's okay. I just wanted to say I am sorry about this week. It's been rough on me and I think I just overreacted but I felt betrayed. After worrying that everyone was against me I never thought you were and then I saw Jonathon Strand at your house and I just ran with that."

"You saw him here?" Charley's smile wasn't what Riley had expected. "That means you had come to see me."

"Well, yeah but I jumped to conclusions and I'm sorry."

"Don't be. I didn't know he was coming over. He just wanted to talk me into some big business deal he's putting together and he's going to find out he trusted the wrong person with details."

"What do you mean?"

"I'll explain it later. I'm just glad we're okay."

"We're okay," Riley nodded. "I'd better get out of here, let you rest."

"I'll see you Wednesday at the auction," Charley said.

"Auction?"

"The bachelor auction?" Charley said, his tone of tenderness towards Riley who'd clearly forgotten something major.

It all came to him then. "That is this week, isn't it." The bachelor auction was held once a year to help the Ladies Garden Club raise funds for the school. Riley and several of the other council members were always there.

Charley nodded. "Good thing I said something."

Riley smiled, embarrassed that he'd forgot. "I've had a lot on my mind," he offered as his pathetic excuse. Charley didn't question it.

They took a few steps, heading back to Annette, then Charley stopped again. "Was that Greg on the phone the other night at the hospital?"

Greg.

"It was," Riley smiled sadly, covering his hurt. "Um, we're officially done."

"I'm sorry. I know that hurt."

"It's best." He said the words but didn't really believe them or it wouldn't still hurt, even after the nice evening he'd just had.

Charley reached up and petted Riley's arm then quickly stopped, like he couldn't trust himself to stop with a simple touch. "I am sorry."

"Thanks. Thanks for tonight. I had fun."

"Good. That's my goal."

"I know. Food, fun and friends."

Charley smiled at him sweetly, so many unspoken words clear in his eyes.

Tornado

It was Greg moving on him that morning. "I LOVE THIS MAN!" Greg was yelling as he held Riley close to him. They were at the mall. Greg's kiss was warm, hungry. Riley felt so happy to have him in his arms once again, knowing this time his lover was there to stay. They would finally have the relationship Riley wanted for them. Finally, everything was perfect.

The dream only brought new sadness to him as he woke up and knew he had to let go of the happiness he felt. It wasn't true and would never be.

In that mood for the day, he instantly got mad as he went to his parking space and found Chief Russell standing there, waiting for him. "What's happened now?" Riley asked, shutting the truck's door. Damn his dad. Not even out of the hospital a week and already back to his old ways.

Chief stepped aside and Riley saw his reserved parking sign. He read the spray painted words that now decorated the sign. "The Best Darn" now sat above the "Mayor".

"The best darn mayor," Chief said, smiling with pride like he'd done the deed himself. "I think it's true."

Riley couldn't hide his smile, kicking himself for having expected something bad from his dad.

"I don't think I'll fine him for this," Chief said, beginning to walk away, "until there's ever a new mayor."

"Thanks, chief," Riley said, offering his friend a wave.

Driving home that night, the storm clouds were fierce in the sky. There had been talk of the severe storms all day, having already produced several tornadoes in its trek there.

Seville County was used to tornadoes. They had seen their share of the storms but it had been years since they'd seen any major damage. The storm clouds moving in that afternoon caught Riley's attention but he didn't think any more of them than usual. All he expected from the stormy night was a phone call from Charley who would be frightened by the intense storms but that was all that bothered his mind.

Charley's call came just minutes after a tornado warning was issued for the next county. In all his years, he had never been in a tornadic storm.

"Don't go anywhere," Riley advised after Charley wanted to come there. "You have a basement, right? Go down in it. Take your cell phone and a pillow or blanket. Take a flashlight. You'll be okay."

"Alright. I'm going now. Call me when it's safe, okay?"

Riley promised he would, smiling at being needed. Charley trusted him completely and he sorta liked that.

He had his own troubles to take care of first. He hurried outside to ensure the horses were loose in the fields and not up by the barn. He got the dogs inside, shutting them in the bathroom while he searched out a flashlight. There was definitely a storm coming. There was an eerie green tint to the air outside and the clouds looked ominously over the area.

He called Tom to see if Tom wanted to come there. His response was the same as with every storm, "What do I have to lose?"

"Your life?"

"Olive will be there."

"And me? I'd like to still see you."

"I know, son. I'll be fine. Lived here thirty-seven years and been okay."

The odds didn't seem to favor that but Riley let it go.

It was within the hour that the storms hit. Riley had his police scanner going, listening to Chief Russell, his officers and the sheriff's deputies out in the storm.

As the storm around him intensified, Riley decided to take cover himself. He was shutting the door to the bathroom and trying to calm the dogs when he heard a bizarre sound outside he wasn't prepared for.

He'd always expected the sound of a train coming but he hadn't expected the high pitch squeal that he just couldn't place to any other sound. He was frozen trying to place the sound when the electricity went out and that sudden end to all around him scared him more than the tornado he knew to be outside.

He slammed the door and prepared himself for his house to be destroyed around him. Trapped in the darkness, the sounds outside were terrifying. He wasn't sure what had been hit but debris was landing on the roof. The wind was ferocious and loud. There didn't seem to be so much storm as just the weird sounds of his house creaking and stuff falling against it that wasn't rain.

And then it was over.

All that was left was the darkness and an unnerving gentle rain that didn't fit with the monster rain that had been.

He stayed in the room a bit longer, then decided it was safe to go out. Curiosity was getting the better of him. Something had been destroyed and he prayed it hadn't been his barn.

The dogs ran with him as he went outside. The dark sky was beginning to ease up allowing Riley to easily see his smaller shed turned upside down and caved in. One wall of it laid against the side of his house. His four-wheeler was still inside the building, upside down as well. The lawn mower, however, rested upright near the truck, as if it'd been sucked out of the shed and placed gently out of the way. The truck looked undamaged, just really clean as the power-spray of the rain had washed all the dirt off.

Everything else seemed to be in place other than tree limbs scattered throughout the fields and yard. The hay field lay flat at one corner where the tornado had tracked through, but then it seemed to head back up into the sky and nothing else was touched.

Riley stood frozen in his spot, unable to believe what had just happened. In all his years living there, he'd never been touched so closely by a tornado.

A gentle breeze blew his shirt and hair as he walked to the gate by him. He began to whistle for his horses, so afraid that they wouldn't all come to him. His concentration was on the empty field, listening for the first sounds of hooves.

A car's approach down the road was all he could hear though. Turning that direction, Riley could see the lights of a cop car before he could see the actual car. By the speedy approach, he knew it was Kevin Russell behind the wheel.

Riley offered a wave as Russell pulled in to let him know he was okay.

"Damn," Kevin said as he got out. "You got lucky."

The night had all felt like a dream to him then and didn't seem to touch his reality. "Is it bad out there?"

The chief nodded. "I was really coming to see if you'd want to go patrol the damage. You're going to be busy with getting disaster relief."

"Anyone hurt?"

The chief shrugged. "I haven't heard of any deaths yet, but there's injuries. A whole neighborhood was hit pretty hard." Kevin nodded back behind Riley, "At least they look fine."

Riley turned to face his beloved horses all running towards him from deep down in the field. He let out a deep relieved sigh. "Thank God."

The sight of the debris was what Riley was used to seeing on the news of tornadoes, he'd just never expected it to be in his town, to recognize the faces of the victims. The damage at his farm was nothing compared to the places where houses were simply gone.

He did his best to help the people there, being anything from a medic to a shoulder to cry on to holding the flashlight so a rescue worker could move into the dark pile of rubble and pull a crying child from it.

The news crews were arriving causing some of Russell's officers to direct traffic full-time. Riley hadn't paid much attention to what was going on outside their debris world until one woman yelled at him.

"Mayor Halleran!"

He turned to the voice but his eyes stopped on a familiar face approaching him with his crew in tow. Greg Robbins looked towards him, but didn't meet his eyes.

The woman's crew was on him first with her questions. Greg's cameraman recorded him as well. Riley reported on what he knew, what the town was offering for victims, and became the face of a small-town mayor out helping his people.

He pretended Greg wasn't there.

But then the interview was over and the crews were separating to film the rescue efforts and the debris. Riley found himself standing before a quiet Greg.

He decided not to be the one that would make it better that time. "I've got work to do," he said and turned away.

"Wait," Greg called, stepping closer to him as he stopped and turned back to face Greg. "I heard your place was hit too. Are you okay?"

"I am. It's okay there. Not like this."

"I'm glad. I was worried."

"Thanks," he said after a few moment's thought, unsure what to say.

Greg took another step towards him like he meant to hug him, but he caught himself and moved away. "I had to come," he said, looking at the ground.

"Shouldn't you be getting ready to leave on vacation?" he asked, hoping his anger sounded through. *Our vacation?*

Greg looked at him and said nothing.

Riley nodded, "I'll see you around." He turned away once again but Greg stepped up to his side. He stopped once more, facing Greg but he didn't look at him. "What is it you want?" Riley said, his voice low. Greg's presence was starting to hurt.

"I need to…" he started but his words faltered.

"Mayor!" Chief Russell said, hurrying to Riley's side. "Can you come look at this?"

"Sure." Riley looked at Greg, seeing a different look in Greg's eyes that he didn't like. Perhaps Greg was thinking he'd made the wrong choice but he wasn't acting on it or apologizing for it, so Riley walked away from him, letting the Chief lead him to some unknown.

They walked for a while before Kevin said anything. "I don't really have anything to show you. I just wanted to get you out of that."

Riley looked back to see Greg was at the news truck, helping the crew load up. "Thanks."

Kevin patted his arm. "I never liked him," he said.

Riley nodded, offering another soft-spoken thanks, dismissing the chief. He stood in the hurting neighborhood, wrapping his arms around himself like he was suddenly cold.

He took a moment to start his phone calls he hadn't done. His dad and Tom were both okay. He called Charley last.

"*That* was cool," Charley said in pure character.

Bachelor Auction

The auction was a big deal in that town. The winning bidder won dinner with the man they'd "bought". Riley didn't mind to offer himself but there was always the fear that no one would bid on him. He knew he could count on Annette who was always in the audience, ready to bid her $50.00 for him if no one else bid. It was still as a nerve-wrecked mess that he took the stage with the school's coach and principal and a few firefighters and Chief Russell, even though the chief had gotten married a few months before.

That night as he scanned the audience, he saw the regular ladies and Charley in full character but it was another familiar face that made his heart speed up. Greg stood towards the back of the room, standing out of the way like he didn't want to be seen. But Riley saw him. He was there and would bid on Riley and win Riley's heart all over by doing such a brave act.

Riley's attention was on him all night. Greg offered a few nervous smiles but stayed out of the way most of the night. When it was Riley's turn, he knew that his life was all about to fall into place and the man of his heart was about to sweep him off his feet.

He didn't really hear what the MC was saying about him. He only saw Greg taking a few steps up, like he intended to be in the game. He wasn't aware of anything else going on in the room other than waiting for Greg's first move.

The bidding had started. The ladies in the front had been offering up amounts and Riley had thanked them, attentive to the whole crowd, but his mind was on Greg. What a great moment it was going to be when he outbid them all.

But Greg wasn't saying anything.

Riley looked at him and saw that Greg was anxiously looking around the room. It seemed like a few times he meant to call out something but his bids never came. After a few tense minutes, he bowed his head and seemed to give up.

Riley's heart fell. He hoped he was covering it up though, with all the attention on him. Then a familiar deep voice got cheers from the room and Riley forced his smile to be genuine as Charley Claremont bid $3,000 and the bidding for him was over.

It was a mix of pure anger and hurt that kept Riley quickly pacing the back room, out of the eyes of the celebration in the main room. Had Greg done that on purpose? Showing up there, knowing that Riley would be glad to see him and expect something when he'd merely been playing him, taking another chance to stab him in the heart.

Charley stepped into the room like he knew to be delicate with his arrival. He must have known Greg had been there. "Are you okay?"

"Okay?" Riley laughed. "How could you do that?" he asked, turning his anger towards Charley even though he knew it wasn't the celebrity's fault. "Why didn't you let Greg have a chance?"

"I let him have a chance," Charley said, his tone changing to meet Riley's. "I let him have several chances. I made only one bid at the end. I didn't counter his bid. He didn't say a word!"

Riley turned away, wanting so desperately to be away from that place but not emotionally stable enough that he wanted to be seen. He could only pace. He wanted to hit something.

"Rie," Charley's tone was more concerned, "I'm sorry. He didn't do anything."

"I know that!" he snapped. Why couldn't he just get what he really wanted for a change? "He should have won, though. I wanted him to win, you know that." Riley faced Charley, again blaming him for Greg's failure.

"I know you did, but sweetheart, he froze up out there. He's not about to fight for you and I'm here ready to shout it from the mountains that I love you. You'd rather love a shadow than be with a real man. You need to realize that he is never going to be anything for you. You need to let tonight be his loss and move on!"

"I'm not ready to. I can't just shut my heart off."

"I don't think it's your heart you're thinking with," Charley dared. "And it's not your brain either. You know how awful he treats you. You know how awful your relationship has been the whole time. You're not half a person, Rie. You deserve to have a man that can be at your side all the time, through good and bad, not just when his pants get an itchin'."

Riley's anger disappeared, leaving behind only the hurt that once again Greg had inflicted. He couldn't look at Charley, couldn't tell him that he was right. "I can't stay here," he said. "I'm sorry. You'll have to finish out the night without me."

Charley nodded, understanding. "I'll tell them you didn't feel good or something."

Riley hurried out of the room, looking only at the floor as he fled the whole scene. He hadn't seen Greg standing in the hallway near the room where Charley remained.

It took Riley several hours to calm down and to let the starkness of his heartbreak fade away. Greg wasn't the man worthy of his waiting, he knew that. He'd just expected too much that evening and been disappointed like he always was.

The worst part of that night was his behavior towards Charley, he knew that too.

He called when he thought Charley might be home after the rest of the evening's events.

Charley answered, his tone cautious. "Yes?"

"I just wanted to apologize. My problems aren't your fault. I'm sorry I took it out on you."

"Rie, I understand. Tonight was a lot for you and there was a lot affecting you. I wasn't considerate enough to see that. I was being selfish."

"No. You were justified. Like I said, you're not the cause of my problems. What happened is between Greg and me. I'm sorry and I owe you a dinner date. Would Friday be okay? I wouldn't have to think about work the next day and it'd be easier for me."

"Certainly. I look forward to it."

Riley sighed, wishing that his words would really erase whatever horrible feelings he'd left Charley with.

"I'll pick you up," Charley added quick, like he knew to keep the conversation on light topics. "Say seven? I promise to have you home early, as well."

"Alright. I'll see you Friday."

He'd made his anxiety stay at bay all week but Friday night he couldn't stop it. He had a date with Charley. He had a *date*.

Tom was there to help, like a proud father. "You just have fun tonight. Don't think. Don't analyze. Just enjoy. It's a pre-arranged date, that's all."

"I'm so nervous. I don't think I was this nervous before my first speech."

"It'll be okay," Tom patted his back, looking at them in the mirror. "I feel like I'm sending you off on Prom night."

"I feel sorta like a scared teenager."

"You'll be fine. No matter what happens, just have fun. You'll be okay," Tom said, smiling sweetly at him.

Riley shrugged. "Can I confess something? I'm sorta looking forward to this. I haven't been on a date in how many years?" he smiled.

One Found, One Lost

Charley arrived a few minutes early. He was dressed in a nice suit, his hair neat. The make-up around his eyes made them shine as he looked upon Riley.

Charley nodded at Tom before they left. "I'll have him home early," he smiled.

As they walked to the car, Charley explained his plans for the evening. "I thought we'd go to the city and eat. I'm not about to attempt to cook anything myself if we want to eat and this way neither of us have to work."

"That's fine." Riley went to the driver's side with Charley and opened it for him. It brought a big smile to Charley's face and lit his eyes even more. Riley watched as Charley got in, thinking that there was no way he could ever be *her man*. Charley might have a feminine persona, but he was a man of strength and confidence. Troubles didn't stick to him. He seemed to be indestructible and untouchable. It was with genuine love that he was escorting Riley to dinner.

How could Riley compare to that?

The restaurant was expensive and elegant. They made an entrance despite Charley's low-key arrival. He was known in the cooking world and he was known in the celebrity world. Yet while Charley was getting the attention, he moved to make sure Riley was at his side.

"I like this place," Charley said after they'd been seated and drinks ordered. "The food is good. The service is great. No one bothers me."

"I can't imagine what it's like to never be able to just eat dinner without someone watching you or coming up to talk to you."

"It took a few years for me to reach that status and it was strange. Generally, I don't have too much trouble."

"Not you," Riley smiled in his tease, "you always seem to be controlling the attention instead of receiving it."

Charley's face lit with a cute smile, not denying his words. "I can't help it. But tonight is all about you, about us. I'm not on show tonight."

"I don't mind. It's strange for me to be eating dinner with someone, really. We never did anything like this," he said, implying Greg.

"Since we're on that subject, um, can I say that Greg and I had words the night of the auction?"

"You did? I didn't know."

"It was after you left. I don't know if you saw him. I guess he'd come back to talk to you and overheard us, well, what I said. He saw you leave but he just stood there and let you leave. He was in the hallway when I left the room. You know me and my mouth. I couldn't just walk away so I said some things I thought he needed to hear."

"Like what?"

"That he was a fool and if he hurt you again I'd make it a point to ruin his life. Oh, I used some different words than that but you get the idea. I just hated seeing you so upset and he's just standing there like a dork that didn't know why."

"Well," Riley said, trying to sum up all the emotions that news was swirling. "I didn't know that. He never called to explain anything."

"I don't want to change the mood of the night. I just don't want you to ever think I'm keeping secrets from you. I wasn't nice to him."

"Greg and I are history. I'm not going to let myself step back into that, even if he did ever try, which he won't. You were right that night. I need to move on. So, I'm here. We're having a nice dinner. That subject is done. He's not going to upset me anymore and I'm terribly sorry I was so hateful to you. I just wanted to keep hope alive that he might still want me," he paused. "I'm glad you won. You did nothing wrong and I'm sorry if I made you feel that you did. I will not be that emotional mess any more."

Charley smiled, reaching over to give Riley's hand a squeeze.

"Good evening," the waiter said, drawing their attention away from their contact.

Charley was slow in releasing Riley's hand, having no guilt at being caught holding it. "Good evening, Richard. We are having a special dinner tonight. What do you recommend?"

The waiter then listed off their specials and his favorite meal there. They ordered and then once the waiter left found themselves in a quietness.

They soon fell into talk about Charley's show he'd just taped and his trip to California. They were interrupted only once by a nice-looking young man coming over. Charley smiled at him, offering a hand for the man who raised it up to a kiss. "Good evening, Miss Claremont," the man smiled. "I just wanted to check on your dinner so far. Everything fine for you and your guest?"

"Oh yes, thank you. This is my date, Riley Halleran. This is the owner, Rick Todds."

Riley shook the man's hand, "Nice to meet you."

"If there is anything you need tonight, just ask," Rick smiled, like he knew this date was something special. Riley felt special at just having been introduced. Charley wasn't hiding why they were there and he liked that.

After dinner, they drove around the town for awhile, neither mentioning the fact it was getting late and they should start heading for home. It was only when they drove past the ice skating rink that Riley spoke up. "Wanna go ice skating?"

The rink wasn't too crowded at that late hour. Riley found the sight of the two of them in their suits and skates a bit humorous, but nothing compared to the fact that neither of them knew how to skate. Arm-in-arm, they helped each other around the rink. Charley, a man so graceful in heels, was at total odds with the skates and leaned on Riley a lot to keep himself from falling.

It wasn't long before they felt brave enough to put some distance between them and soon they were skating independently. Their talk hadn't ended though, continuing to share stories of their lives and getting to know the other. There were just a few times one would be talking and then realize the other had fallen down. Helping each other stand back up was an experience that brought them laughter and by the end of it all their stomach muscles hurt worse than their fallen-on butts.

The drive home was relaxing. There was no traffic on the highway, just a clear night showing the stars and brilliant full moon. Riley laid his head back in the seat, watching the night's sky through the sunroof. Nice music played quietly in the background, another one of Charley's obscure musical likes that was perfect for the late night drive. While they'd shared hours of stories, they were both quiet then, enjoying the simple moment.

At Riley's house, they remained in the car a few minutes more. "Do you want to come in? Have a drink?"

"I should get home, let you get some sleep. I will take a good-night kiss, though," he smiled. "Just a simple one," he said, turning his cheek to Riley.

Riley gave him a light kiss, amused. "I had a good time tonight. Thank you."

"I did, too. Let me walk you up. It's the proper thing to do."

They left the car and met at the front of it. They walked to the house in silence. Riley tried to decide whether he'd let something more happen if Charley did chose to come in or if he'd be okay with the night ending at the doorway. He suspected Charley was going through the same debate.

But the door was in front of them and it was time for decisions.

"Good night, Rie," Charley said, moving in to kiss his cheek.

"Good night. Be careful going home," he added, seeing that Charley really wasn't staying.

"Can I call you tomorrow?"

"Please."

"Have sweet dreams," Charley smiled.

Charley had been gone for some time and Riley had changed his clothes and gotten ready for bed but he couldn't sleep and he knew it. He'd had too great a night. All he could think of was calling Tom to let him know what a fantastic night it had been and let his friend and father figure know that for a change, he was completely happy.

The Funeral and the Lovers

Riley's morning started a bit late. He hadn't been able to sleep and then had slept in that next morning. Tom hadn't called to see where he was so he felt it was okay to take the morning a bit slower. Tom probably suspected his night was still going on, perhaps with company there.

He took a shower and got dressed for the day, wondering if Charley would call soon or later that afternoon or if he'd call Charley first. It was a thought that made him smile.

Tom never answered his phone that morning. He couldn't get over how strange that was, since he'd no doubt be wanting to know how the date went, but he thought Tom might just have been outside working. After he ate, he drove by to see if Tom was in the garage or out in the yard.

The house was dark though, making Riley's heart fill with a fear that it was about to be hurt. He pulled in and parked behind Tom's truck. He went to the door and knocked and rang the bell. He waited and listened to sounds inside to see if Tom was just moving slow.

Deciding it all wasn't good, Riley tried his key in the door but found the chain held as the door opened. Stepping back, he slammed himself into the door and forced it to open. He'd gladly pay to have the door fixed, he thought as he stepped inside the quiet house, instead of face what his instinct was trying to tell him.

His calls were only met with silence. He went to the bedroom and felt his skeleton take two steps back while his body remained in its place as he looked into the room.

Tom was sleeping in his bed, or at least he looked like he was. The color about his face wasn't that of a sleeping man though. "Oh, Tom…"

Riley felt his eyes tearing up as he moved to the phone in the living room. He fought to deny his emotions to surface, denying himself to feel anything other than to follow the protocol that had to be. He called Chief Russell's office to report it then standing in Tom's living room, looking around at items of Tom's life that were mere items then, Riley realized there was no one else to call.

The funeral was a few days later. Only a handful of mourners showed up at Tom's grave side. They all seemed to be there for Riley and concerned about him more than grieving Tom. Charley arrived last. He watched as Charley parked and then stepped out.

Charley was dressed in a dark suit, there as the man he was, not the character the town knew. There was no make-up, no show. He tugged at his jacket's front as he walked towards Riley, as if he was nervous, but he offered a sad smile.

Riley stepped out to meet him, stepping into Charley's hug. "Thanks for coming."

Charley nodded as they parted. "Tom was a great soul. I want to honor him." Tears filled Charley's eyes but he didn't move to acknowledge them. "And you. I want to be here for you."

"Thank you." Riley quickly rubbed Charley's arm, offering a small dose of comfort and then moved to let Charley take a seat.

The service was brief. The preacher said a few words. Riley delivered the eulogy. Rafe Chapman said a few good words of Tom's history. And then it was over. Tom Watts would be a memory and an empty spot in Riley's life.

He'd eaten dinner only because he felt obligated to after Charley had gone to such trouble but he hadn't really wanted anything. Tom's passing had affected Riley greatly and nothing solidified his loss more than seeing the casket lowered into the ground. It was a haunting image that clung to him and snuffed out any feeling of happiness or peace. Driving past Tom's place had brought tears to his eyes. Tom was really gone.

Charley had been caring that night, not saying too much, careful not to trouble Riley's distant mind. He'd fixed dinner because he'd felt that was his purpose there, he'd explained. He hadn't tried to cheer Riley up with false sentiment, merely allowed him the distance to experience whatever he needed to and yet be there if he was needed.

Watching Charley clean up the dinner dishes filled Riley with a strange thought that made him sad. He knew how much Tom would have loved to see Charley and Riley together, able to comfortably move through dinner and the night.

He felt bad that his eyes filled with tears and had wanted to hide them from Charley but he couldn't. Charley smiled sweetly at him as he moved to him with an offering of tissues.

"I've never felt so alone," Riley confessed. "Tom was like the last of my family. Who do I have now in this huge world?"

"I'd be willing to volunteer," Charley said with no hint of hurt in his tone. "Your dad is out there."

"Well, that's not much though."

Charley sat at his side. "If it helps any? In all the people that I know and can call friends or family or such, I have only you and your dad. I don't have real friends. If Charley Claremont was suddenly a nobody, do you think any of them would answer my calls?"

He thought about Charley's words, aware that he believed that claim. He raised his glass, which Charley raised his glass to, "Then here's to the three of us." They toasted and drank.

"I bet Tom and Olive are up there right now dancing the night away or something else if that's allowed. He missed her so much. It's good they're together. I'm not much substitute for that. He's happy, so I'll be happy."

Charley raised his glass again, "To Tom and Olive."

"Tom and Olive." They drank.

Riley's eyes locked on Charley's. They both held the moment then Charley moved nervously away. "Well, I should head for home," he said, taking his glass to the kitchen.

Riley followed him, leaning against the cabinet. "I do appreciate all you did today. Dinner was great."

"You need to eat. I know you don't feel like it, but you still have to eat."

"Thank you for being here for me," he nodded. "I do need someone to take care of me sometimes."

"My pleasure," Charley smiled, his smile more the character he was.

Riley sat his glass down and then went to hug Charley. "Thank you," he whispered and then stepped back, but he found himself stopping just before he left Charley's hold. It wasn't a decision he'd made, but he found himself acting it out.

He stepped closer to Charley and moved to lightly kiss his lips. The light kiss turned into another one and then one more and then their lips parted and the kiss had a life of its own.

"Oh, honey," Charley sighed, leaning his head against Riley's after breaking from the kiss, "I've been dreaming about that."

Riley hugged him again, holding him for a long moment. He moved back but they stayed in the hold. "Do you want to stay the night?"

"Do I *want* to?" Charley laughed. "Yes, and no. Yes, obviously because I want to. No, because you might just be emotionally upset and not sure what you want."

"I'm not emotionally upset. I just don't want you to go home. It's late and dark and your car has a history of flat tires," he smiled.

"Ooohhhh," Charley smiled, appearing to be honestly nervous about Riley's offer.

"We don't have to do anything. Just stay. We don't want to be alone. You've taught me to be honest to myself and I don't want you to go."

"Then I won't," Charley smiled, lightly kissing Riley. "Will you still respect me when you see me out of character?"

"Is that what you're worried about? This is who you are, isn't it? You don't have the make up on. What's to change?"

"Well, I mean I'm all savvy and classy and you're making me fumble through this like a school girl."

Riley smiled, stepping close to him and kissing his lips, deciding their talking wasn't going to solve anything. He'd doubted before that he could ever be man enough for Charley, but as they kissed, he saw the facade of strength slip away and the truly vulnerable soul Charley was exposed. Charley melted into him.

They didn't speak, just stealing kisses as they moved to Riley's bed. They undressed each other, kissing and touching, neither rushing the moment that was leading to more, just enjoying.

Riley moved inside him, loving Charley's body. The sound of Charley's moans excited him even more, this man of strength allowing him to be part of his vulnerability and sharing his body. Charley laid beneath him, his legs spread wide, his eyes closed tight, his mouth open ready to receive kisses or let moans out, sharing his private ecstasy with him. Riley kissed him hungrily, willing to be swallowed up by Charley if it was possible.

They had slept some. A shower together that early morning had landed them back in bed. Charley laid over Riley, controlling the kisses and leading them. He landed his kisses on the small of Riley's back. He laid over him, moving his kisses up Riley's back to his neck as he moved to take him. Charley slid his fingers between Riley's and squeezed his hand as he slowly made love to him.

It was the most romantic and fulfilling love making Riley had ever experienced, the teddy bear of a lover over him, holding him and tender with him. He fell even more in love with Charley during the sweet and slow passionate moment.

Charley slid his hands under him as they shared the silence after, remaining above him and lightly kissing Riley's cheek. "I love you," Charley whispered, merely out of breath to make his declaration any louder.

Riley smiled, closing his eyes and wrapping himself even more in Charley's hug, "I love you, too."

Riley's Family

It was late Thursday morning when Riley woke. Charley was curled up to him, awake and softly humming a sweet tune. His fingers lightly stroked Riley's chest. A gentle roll of thunder passed over the house making Riley smile. The moment couldn't be any more perfect, he thought.

He laid his hand on Charley's head, letting his love know he was awake.

Charley raised up and lightly kissed his lips. Their kiss grew but remained only a kiss.

"We need to eat," Charley smiled once they'd parted.

"Can we eat in bed?"

"Don't you think we should get out of here sometime?"

"Not before Monday."

Charley stared at him, like he was gathering thoughts that he wasn't sure how to speak.

"What?" Riley asked.

Charley looked down at him, petting his hair and cheek. "I want you to know that you are the first person to really make me nervous. I can talk to anybody but you make me feel like an idiot almost. The day at the café, that I gave you the sculpture? It took me a minute to find the nerve to come to your table."

"Well, no one would know," he said, surprised. "I sure didn't. You're always so confident, always say the right thing."

"I just use my humor to get me out of it when I do say the wrong thing. I'm a clown. I want people to laugh at me. How messed up is that."

"You are the sweetest clown I know," Riley smiled, rolling onto him and kissing him.

"I just want to impress you," Charley said, cupping Riley's cheek in his hand. "I'm afraid I'll screw it up and lose you forever."

"I'm the one screwing it up. I'm glad I didn't make you too mad. I wouldn't want to lose you, either." He lightly kissed Charley, grinding his hips against him, making it clear he meant to spend the rest of the week and weekend in that bed with him. "Besides, you're the first man I've ever called in sick for."

"You are sick," Charley said, all serious. "Sick and should stay in bed definitely."

Whatever late morning romp could have started, it lost out to Charley's hunger. They got up, dressing to some degree since people had the habit of coming over unannounced. Riley slid on his robe and Charley put on his bikini underwear and a tee-shirt. Unable to resist, Riley watched Charley walk by and noticed how muscular his legs were. They were long and very feminine when he wore heels, but just fresh out of bed, Riley noted the strength to them.

Charley stopped, aware Riley was staring at him. "Something wrong?"

"No," he smiled. "Just admiring." He went to where Charley stood and slid his arms around him. "You're beautiful," he whispered then kissed Charley.

Charley's breakfast he fixed that morning was just something quick. He didn't want to concentrate on cooking and he didn't want to keep them out of bed long. Riley sliced fruit while Charley fixed eggs and toast. They planned to load up their plates and head back to bed.

He hadn't been looking to see whatever had caused Charley to let out a quick scream but then the doorbell rang.

"Someone walked by," Charley reported, startled from having been watching out the front window as the visitor walked by.

"Who?" Riley asked, going to the door. He figured it was someone coming to check on him. His office had understood his calling in, knowing how much Tom had meant to him, but there might still be a concern about him being alone. But who he found at the door was more of a surprise.

Rennick Halleran stood at the door, offering a "Hey," as Riley opened the door.

"Hey," he replied, not too sure what to say. "Um, come in." Might as well get the announcing over with, he thought. If his dad had a problem with them being together, he could leave. Win-win either way.

"They told me you'd called in sick," Rennick said as he stepped inside, "That's not like you so I tried calling Charley but he didn't call back so I got worrying and I saw his car here," he reported then looked up as Charley stepped out of the kitchen. "Oh,"" he said, looking upon Charley in his bikinis and tussled hair. "But I guess everything is fine."

"Sorry," Riley said, feeling really awkward, "I didn't know you'd be worried."

"Well," he smiled, probably embarrassed about his march over there then, "I'm proud of you, actually. Ditchin' work to play around. Wow. That's so not you."

Riley smiled, aware he was beginning to like the new Riley. "Have you had breakfast?"

"Well, I don't want to interrupt anything."

"Nonsense," Charley waved a hand at him. "There's plenty to eat and we've got to rest up anyway," he said, leaving the room and Riley embarrassed.

The three sat at the table, eating, sharing small talk. Riley noted how comfortable it was suddenly, his dad and his lover both there. He felt like a real family for a change.

"I heard ole Strand offered to buy ole Webb's farm out off Cutler Road," Rennick mentioned late into their breakfast.

Riley shook his head, so sick of that man's presence. "I hope they said no."

"Oh yeah, for now. Who knows how long any farmer can hang on. Well, *you* know how hard it is. Depends on when the farmer can't take anymore. Money speaks loudly when the time is right."

Riley sighed, beginning to lose his appetite. Strand had probably come to visit him that one day just to scope out his farm, mentally figure up what price he would offer Riley when the time came. "I'd never sell to Strand, no matter how desperate. That man just…," he started but let his sentence stop. He looked at Charley, "You never did tell me what Strand was doing at your place that one day."

"Well," Charley smiled, laying the fork on the plate and quickly glancing at Rennick, "he was just trying to sucker me into his land deal he had going. He's looking for business partners," Charley and Rennick shared a smile. "He intends to buy Kelley's farm and my place is close enough to it that if I wanted to, I could go in it with him."

"In what? What's this between you two? You make me nervous."

"Do you know of the Village Law?" Rennick asked.

"Sorta. It's not really used anymore."

"He plans to use it."

"Oh," Riley sighed, feeling defeated and crushed. "That's how he'd get around our zoning laws."

"Declares his land its own village, suddenly the county laws no longer apply. He could put whorehouses out there if he wanted to."

He shook his head, feeling nauseous. "How can we stop that?"

He saw Charley and Rennick exchange another look that didn't make him feel better. "I don't want you two getting into trouble. He's already out to prosecute."

"We're not," they said at the same time.

"I'll just say," Charley spoke up, "that it was good that he approached me with that offer and as far as he knows I'm not much into land dealings and all this legal stuff. He just happen to be telling too much stuff to the wrong person," Charley smiled.

"What are you two planning?"

His two troublemakers just smiled at him.

"Aw, wait," Charley said, quickly getting out of bed and streaking through the bedroom. "I've gotta brush my teeth," he explained as he disappeared into the bathroom.

Riley laid back in bed, smiling at the humorous image of Charley.

He soon returned with the same rush to his steps, getting back under the covers. "Better. Too much garlic at dinner," he winced, moving over Riley.

"I'm not a vampire," he smiled, "I don't mind."

Charley licked Riley's lips, a minty flavor to his kiss.

"But that is nice," Riley said dreamingly.

The sun was beginning to set, dimming the light in the room, but he could still see Charley's face. He ran his fingers over it, studying his lover's face. "I know it's bad to get serious, but what happens after Sunday when the real world sneaks back in on us?"

Charley looked at him, collecting thoughts, moving one hand to stroke Riley's face the way Riley did his. "Well, I'm sure our bodies will be glad for the rest."

"I'm serious. Your life is all celebrities and traveling and touring. I can't do that."

"I won't have to travel too much. And if I do, I'll make sure I'm here every weekend. No different than what we'd do now. Work five days. Too tired to do anything until the weekend. We'll just be sleeping alone for five days and exhausted from two days of endless sex."

"And I'm supposed to believe a life like you is going to be faithful?"

"I will cut my dick off and leave it here with you until I get back if you wish."

"That's not possible."

"Might be. I haven't tried," he said, being coy, but then got serious. "I don't know what I can promise. Let's just see where it goes. I'm not going to hurt you, Riley. I came here to heal your wounds and bring you happiness and life. I don't hurt people and you don't either. I witnessed that first hand. You were going to let me get away because of a wishful desire for a man that couldn't have you. I know you'll be true. I vow to live up to the same."

"It's a chance I'll have to take, huh?"

"Chance," he said, getting bedroom eyes. He moved to lay on Riley then kissed his lips. He moved down to his neck, nibbling there as Riley arched his body towards Charley's.

"You never told me the story of the painting," Riley said, thinking of the painting only as he closed his eyes during Charley's nibbles and the painting flashed before him.

"It us," Charley replied, taking one of Riley's nipples into his mouth and sucking on it a bit before letting Riley go.

"Us?" He lifted Charley's chin to look into Charley's pretty eyes.

"I am the orange and you are the yellow. It is our souls, our bodies, our lives blending together. Red and white for definition but could be," Charley said, moving back so his lips were just almost touching Riley's, "that red is for the heat of passion, may that never run out." He lightly kissed Riley's lips, making Riley long for a deeper kiss. Charley moved back. "It is just a translation of us."

"I love it," Riley whispered, pulling Charley to a deep kiss as Charley moved his leg to find his way to him. Riley raised his hips to Charley, letting the kiss end. He took Charley inside him with a sweet moan, closing his eyes and giving himself over to the passion that had begun.

Greg's Goodbye

It *could* have been Greg's car that Riley had seen in traffic the day before. It *could* have been his ex on the phone that night he'd gotten home and didn't get to the phone in time. Riley didn't know if he was just thinking about him and making it seem like Greg was still around or if he was right in believing Greg was trying to get in touch with him again.

Whatever the case may have been, it was clearly Greg on the phone late that night and Riley wasn't sure what to do. Answer it or let them just fade away? Would there be more anger or pleading to try again? Riley wasn't sure he'd be able to say what he needed to nor was he prepared if Greg wanted a second chance.

He wasn't ready to face what was ahead of him but he answered.

Greg sounded tired perhaps even depressed. He didn't sound like himself. "I just wanted to call and tell you some things," he said, no threat or happiness to his tone. "I'm getting divorced."

"What?" Riley asked, truly surprised. Those had been words he wanted to hear for so long and then there they were and it only made him feel troubled.

"I've lied to everyone for so long. It's time I face up to life and quit letting it just run by me. You were right all this time but I never really understood. I think I needed to see how much I was hurting you before I would let myself understand how wrong my life is. That night you left the auction," he started but let his sentence fade.

"Greg—"

"—No. I needed to see that I was hurting you. That night really opened my eyes and I am truly sorry I've hurt you. I can't be the man up there declaring my love for you and I don't want to be *this* man that has hurt you. So I'm making some changes. I'm going to be moving to New York. I've accepted a job there. I'll be leaving soon but I didn't want to leave this between us."

"You're leaving?" he asked, sitting down as the idea of Greg's complete departure from his life affected him and made his legs weak. He rested his head on his hand and started massaging his temple. He was feeling a new heartbreak but he kept it silent.

"Yeah. I need to be away from my family. I've never been more than five minutes from them all my life. It's time I go on my own. I need to listen to myself and not them. I don't know who I am, Riley. Gay, straight? Newsman or waiter? I don't know. So I'm going to go find out without anyone telling me what to pick."

Riley smiled at Greg's bravery but his heart wasn't sure what to feel.

"I'm scared, Rile," Greg said, sounding like he was smiling to cover up tears. "And this hurts so badly you can't imagine. I've broken so many hearts and now I'm breaking my own."

"It'll be okay," he said, wanting to be strong for his former lover. "Change is hard and it's scary. But, wow, you're doing something fabulous. I think maybe that is what you need. I'm always here if you need to talk."

"Thanks. You are really a great man, Riley. I should have seen that from the beginning and been a great man for you too."

"It's past, Greg. We can't change it. We're where we're supposed to be I think. You'll find that happiness you want too. This will be difficult for you but you're doing a good thing. Don't give up."

"I was excited about it but as it gets closer I'm starting to get more scared."

"That's normal. Just face it, though. You can do it. Before you know it, you'll be in a place that feels so right."

Greg was quiet a moment then in a soft tone asked, "Are you seeing Charley?"

"I am, yes." That admission felt more strange than Riley thought it would.

Greg cleared his throat. "He's very protective of you, very much in love with you."

"I'm sorry about the auction. I don't know what he said."

"Just things I needed to hear. He was right and I do think he's the right man for you."

Riley smiled, his thoughts going instinctively to Charley. "Don't worry about me, okay? I'm happy. You be happy too. You'll find what you're looking for."

Greg was quiet.

Riley closed his eyes, wanting to hug his ex, to hold him and make all his worries go away.

"I love you, Rile. I really do. I always have loved you. I was just a coward. I couldn't be the man you needed me to be no matter how much I wanted to be. So, I'll go do this, find out who I really am. Who knows, maybe I can come back and give Charley the fight for you."

"Maybe," Riley smiled with Greg's tease, knowing it would never be. He would probably never see Greg again. "I love you. You call me if you need to talk or need something, okay? You're not alone out there."

"Thanks. I will. When I get settled, I'll email or call ya. Give you all my new info."

"Okay."

"Riley?" Greg said then paused like his words wouldn't come. "I'm glad you've found someone. You deserve that."

He wasn't sure how to respond to that.

"Okay. Well, I'll talk to you soon then."

"Good luck. Be strong. Have a safe trip," he said, feeling the need to end the polite way. They weren't together. They weren't anything more than friends. "Enjoy."

Making Hay

He felt outnumbered by the enemy that day stepping out of his house with plans to go cut his hayfields by himself. He didn't entertain thoughts of what if the weather didn't cooperate or what if the tractor broke down again or even question how he was going to physically load all the bales and unload them in the barn by himself.

He didn't think. He just merely stepped out into the day with the intention of cutting hay.

He hadn't done much when a sadness came over him. He made a turn in the field expecting to see the second tractor a few rows over following his path. Tom should have been there. Looking out and seeing only the field made his heart fill with loss.

It was within an hour after starting that Riley saw a truck head towards his house and pull in. It was an aggravation he thought about ignoring. He didn't have time to head back to the house and then back to the field just to see what someone wanted. He expected Charley sometime that afternoon with lunch but Riley didn't recognize the truck.

The truck was driving in the upper field towards him. The driver was careful to stay out of the hay, remaining at the edge of the road and Riley's field. Parked even with the tractor, Riley saw his dad and Charley get out. He offered them a confused wave, shutting the tractor down.

He climbed down and headed towards them. "What are you doing?"

His father was dressed in work clothes. Charley was also in jeans and shirt and without makeup like he intended to work.

"You need help," Rennick said. "We're here to help."

"Do what?"

"What would Tom have done?"

"He had a tractor. We'd both do whatever."

"Okay. Where's his tractor? I can follow you. Char here is going to keep us fed."

"Are you sure? It'll be long, hot days. What about your heart?"

Rennick shrugged. "I'm fine. This will keep me out of trouble then, huh? Show me to the tractor."

His dad was true to his word, there every day to cut or rake or bale. Charley kept them hydrated and fed and slept in Riley's arms every night. Riley felt encouraged that he might just pull it off after all.

But the second day of doing the bales, rain clouds were obvious. Riley could feel the rain in the wind. They had a long ways to go to get the hay baled and even then he didn't want it to get wet. He didn't want to think about the hundreds of bales that would be sitting in the fields with only three men and one trailer to collect them.

He ignored the lighting in the distance. He kept going forward. Some hay would be better than none, he told himself. Prices might be higher that year and he might be able to recoup some of the loss that way.

His dad drove the truck while Charley and he got the bales on the trailer. He didn't pay much attention, merely in the mindset of load the bales, load the bales, please don't rain yet, please don't rain yet.

"How did you two do this alone?" Charley complained a few rows in. Charley had started stacking the bales on the trailer while Riley tossed them up to him.

Riley shrugged. "Started out able to afford to hire guys to help me. Used to have conveyors to help," he said in between lifting bales onto the trailer. "They broke so one year we stacked them and then lifted the stacks with a tractor. We've just gotten creative each year. Never the same plan each year."

"I think it's time for a new plan," Charley growled, letting out a tired deep breath.

It wasn't long before a truck honking caught Riley's attention. It was approaching them in the field with a hand waving from the driver's side.

"Who's that?" Rennick asked.

"Bill," Riley said, staring perplexed at the approaching truck that pulled a trailer. He stole a glance at his smiling dad before looking back at Bill and his son getting out of the truck.

"We thought you might want some help," Bill said, shaking Riley's hand strongly and patting his upper arm hard. "I'd been here when you cut too but we didn't get back from vacation in time. Those rain clouds don't look so friendly."

Riley was almost speechless, unsure whether to address Bill first or to find out what his scheming father was up to.

"Alright," Bill said, "we'll start out in the field, work our way to the barn then?"

"Sure," Riley nodded then looked at his dad and Charley. "Did you two put him up to this?"

"No," Rennick said, sounding as surprised as Riley felt.

Bill and his son were almost back to their truck when another truck honked, heading down the road. This time it was his neighbor, Scott Harolds. Scott and his truckload of guys parked down the way and unloaded. Scott walked over to them, offering greetings to Rennick and Charley. "We just finished up ourselves. With that rain comin', thought you might need some help."

With no idea of how much it affected Riley, Scott simply reported that his brother was driving their trailer over and bringing their conveyer. But with the way his brother drove, it might be late afternoon before he got there, he reported, getting a good laugh from all the guys. Scott's brother Michael was known only for his tendency to drive slow no matter what the vehicle.

Riley knew he was participating in the talk and laughter but deep inside he was stuck in a wave of generosity he'd never expected. Charley seemed to know what he was feeling for he smiled sweetly at him.

Another surprise came hours after they'd started working when three car loads arrived at separate times with people offering to help or to bring food and drinks for the crews.

They were unloading the last trailer of square bales when the rain moved into the area and dumped on them.

Riley stood in the storm, surrounded by the people of the town and a barn full of hay. At the end of the long day, Riley bid everyone farewell and a huge amount of thanks. He saw them all off, not caring that he was getting soaked. Rennick had left with a hug and a promise to see him the next day.

Alone again, he moved towards the house.

Charley was asleep on the sofa when Riley walked in. It brought a smile to him to see Charley there.

In a daze, Charley went to bed and was instantly asleep again but Riley couldn't sleep, despite his body's exhaustion. He was still overwhelmed by the amount of help that had arrived on its own accord.

He'd told Charley some time ago that he wouldn't have minded losing everything and starting over but he'd been wrong. The support he'd received that day had saved more than just his hay. It'd saved his love for that town and his home.

"One man *can* make a difference," his dad had said earlier that night before he left.

Riley cuddled Charley up to him, petting Charley's hair, in love with that man more than he had ever imagined he could feel. He was full of the peace in knowing that everything was going to be alright. He wasn't alone in his battles or his life.

He leaned up and lightly kissed Charley's head and then laid still, listening to Charley's deep breaths.

The Auction

But his love and hope were rained on the next week by the reality of Jonathon Strand's plan. Riley had done some research and he could start petitions to get the law overturned, get it on the ballot and let the people vote, all of which would take a year at least. Meanwhile, the farm would have already been plowed under. He might have gotten a cease and desist order while they waited, but with Strand's money and connections, Riley didn't really see that happening.

He went to the auction with a heavy heart and a mind full of hope that lightning would just strike Strand down. Strand arrived soon enough, casting an evil, victorious glare his direction. Riley turned away, sickened by the man's presence.

But Strand was headed towards him. He felt the need of a cross to hold out to protect himself. "Mayor Halleran," Strand smiled, but didn't offer his hand. "I'm glad you're here. You can witness my victory."

He didn't know what to say to that, only thinking that was the perfect moment for the lightning to strike. "It'd only be a victory for you, Mr. Strand," Riley said, hoping to not sound as hateful as he really felt. He wasn't like his father. He didn't want to make a scene.

"I like you," Strand nodded. "You don't back down from a fight. You stand behind your decisions. Smart. Dedicated. These are all qualities I look for in a business partner," Strand paused, probably hoping the words would sink deep into Riley's ego. "I could train you to be a right good businessman. My company needs leaders like you."

"You're offering me a job?" he almost laughed.

Strand nodded. "No sense fighting against each other. Together, we'd be an unstoppable team."

"Wow," Riley smiled, looking around to see Charley's Pacifica pulling up. "Unstoppable," he sighed. "So you'd listen to me then when I said your subdivisions would need to go somewhere else, that people move to the country for the country?"

Strand still smiled but it was different. "There's no money in that."

"No. Just life and tranquility and peace and happiness."

"You're just like your dad," Strand scoffed. "Full of far-fetched concepts and idiotic ideals."

Riley smiled, meeting Strand's eyes. "I hope so," he said, his politeness slipping.

Strand's did as well. "You're again missing your chance at success here. I don't usually give second chances."

"Thanks, but no thanks."

Strand's smile left completely. "I'll be seeing you at *your* farm's auction then."

Riley clenched his teeth as the man walked away, nothing to say, just trying to keep his disgust inside. He let out an deep, angry sigh and decided to look for Charley instead of dwell on Strand's irritation.

But when he spotted Charley and his father, he caught his breath. They would have looked humorous but their arrival struck fear into him.

His dad was dressed in a suit, nicely cleaned up like he was going to a dance. Charley was at his side, dressed in full regalia: a bright orange dress and heels and a large white hat. He wore dark sunglasses but Riley knew he was looking at him for he smiled sweetly.

The two walked arm-in-arm, like a normal couple headed to a polo match. Their entrance could not be ignored.

Riley hurried to their side, stopping their parade. "What are you two up to?"

"Just coming to a real estate auction," Rennick stated, like Riley's question was ridicules.

"No. What are you *up* to?"

"Relax, sweetheart," Charley smiled, reaching a gloved hand out to touch Riley's cheek.

"No. You can't outbid him. He has investors and unlimited finances. Don't do this." There was a brief wave of fear through Riley that his dad had financed their farm to cover this but he quickly pushed that thought away. The two were up to something more.

Charley waved his worry away. "I have the same arsenal, sweet. He, though, has one weakness I don't have."

Rennick leaned up. "Profit margin. He wants to get this for the tax value, not the dollar value. He has a cut-off."

"You said yourself he'd run over you if you stood in his way. He's not going to let this go."

Rennick looked at him oddly. "You on his side now? That what that meeting was about just now?"

"No! But I don't want you to get taken in this deal," he said to Charley.

"I know what I'm doing," Charley said. "Don't worry. He's about to be taken down by..." Charley looked at Rennick, "What'd he call me? An aging, cross-dressing queer reject?"

"He called you that?" Riley gasped.

"Well," Charley winced, "I probably deserved it. I'd just told him to shove his business deal up his, well, you know."

"And it doesn't sit too well that he can't get us for vandalizing his places," Rennick reported, looking at the crowd then back at his son.

Riley closed his eyes, laying his hand over his heart. "Please stop doing that, okay. You two will get in serious trouble."

"We're done, sweet," Charley rubbed his arm. "We're stepping our game up. His two nightmares are about to take his dream away from him."

Riley nodded, thinking for a moment that everything was going to be okay after all. His plan for the lightning wasn't really one they could count on so he'd go with theirs. "You two do look nice by the way."

The two said their thank yous at the same time.

Riley could only shake his head. "He's my boyfriend, right?" he asked his dad, seeing how comfortable the two looked and couplish in their act.

"With my blessing," Rennick smiled.

The three went to stand with the crowd as the auctioneer got ready. Strand stood on the opposite side of them. His expression was one of repulsion and irritation. It only made Riley hate that man more.

The bidding started low. Charley let Strand make the first bid then immediately raised it. The game didn't seem to bother Strand too much, other than force him to hide his embarrassment as the crowd had obviously come to watch the celebrity undermine his plans. Each counter bid was met with giggles or some cheers. Strand kept his expression frozen, not reacting to Charley's actions.

But his stern expression began to slip a shade as each bid took the dollar amount higher and higher and soon at the level that Riley guessed was more than what he was willing to pay. Strand wouldn't back out then, he knew, not wanting to be outdone by a gay, cross-dressing talk show host.

So Strand shouted out a bid probably three times what he'd wanted to pay. The crowd reacted and looked at Charley.

In pure show, Charley winced and then raised his bid a thousand dollars. He blew a kiss Strand's direction.

Strand went ten thousand more, his frustration clear in his voice.

Charley casually raised it.

The battle continued until a ten thousand dollar done-deal went into the millions. It was with anger that Jonathon Strand backed down from a deal. He marched away from the crowd who whooped and cheered.

Riley couldn't believe it was really over. Charley had saved the farm and Riley's town. So happy, Riley grabbed Charley and kissed him, not caring if he had lipstick on him then or if the people cared to see that or not. With the mood of the crowd though, it was just possible they all wanted to give Charley a big kiss.

Riley's Odd Little Town

The crowd was gone. What Patricia Kelley had sold had been moved away and the auctioneer group was loading up their tables and gear and leaving. Soon only Charley, Riley and Rennick were left at Charley's new home.

Charley slid his arm around Riley's waist as they walked towards the house. He took the hat off, complaining at how hot the damn thing had been.

"You do realize you own two farms in a small town far away from California, don't you?" Riley asked, noting that his dad was hanging back from them.

"I do. And I realize that there's a lot of land that will need hay cut and sold and there's a great barn for my tractors and concubines, I mean combines."

"So you're moving here?" Riley asked, not real sure what he expected the answer to be.

"Actually, no. I've arranged for Patricia Kelley to live here as long as she wants."

"You did that?"

Charley smiled at him. "I'm not a complete oblivious hair-brain. I heard she was losing her place. I came to fix her lunch and I just absolutely fell in love with her. So I got thinking and then Strand pissed me off so I thought some more and your dad and I came up with this really nice idea. I've never seen someone so mad," he winced then smiled. "Call *me* names, will you."

"Well, you're smarter than I am. I never thought about you getting involved in this. I wouldn't have been able to ask."

"I know so I just did it. Didn't let you worry about it."

Riley squeezed him, shaking his head. "I can't trust either one of you, can I?"

The diner had been alive with the news when they'd first arrived there but soon it had died down and the three were allowed to eat dinner in peace. Charley had changed from his uncomfortable outfit to his more normal attire. Rennick had wasted no time changing out of the suit for his regular clothes.

There was only a brief moment where the three's mood sagged. They overheard that Webb had sold his place to Strand the week before.

Rennick bowed his head, then spoke up. "We lost one battle," he said, nodding in the direction of the ones talking about Webb. "But we haven't lost the war. We saved a major farm today, won a major victory." A devilish smile came over his face, "And then there's always the Terrible Twosome."

"Oh boy," Riley sighed, visions of the future headaches to be.

Charley reached over and held his hand, giving it a gentle squeeze. Perhaps he was agreeing to not plague Riley's worries or perhaps he was just saying they wouldn't be too terrible on him. Whatever the meaning, Riley liked holding Charley's hand. He was aware any passerby could see. Neither of them let go and no one gave them a second glance.

Riley felt at home in his town, sitting with his trouble-maker father and his celebrity boyfriend. Visions of the Terrible Twosome and the future battles with Strand disappeared into thoughts of his upcoming night with Charley. His life had changed - all for the better. Charley had been right about that. He was a different person. For the first time in a long time, he felt happy.

He looked around the town and at the people around them. He didn't feel like their caretaker any longer but one of them. He had his father back in his life and he had a man that truly loved him and that he loved.

He could only smile as he heard the band begin to play outside the diner, preparing to make their march around the square once again in protest but for Riley it was the perfect ending to a perfect day. Well, almost the perfect ending. Charley's smile foretold what the perfect ending was going to be.

He held Charley's hand to him, leaning in closer to his lover. They watched as the band marched by, followed soon by the police trying to stop them. Mr. Crenshaw drove up the wrong way, headed to lock up his store. People offered friendly greetings to others they passed on the street, some waving in at Riley.

The town's mood felt different to him. It wasn't just his imagination. It was real. Riley couldn't hide his smile. He liked his little odd town.

LaVergne, TN USA
11 April 2010
178824LV00002B/18/P